THE
FORK,
THE
WITCH,
AND THE
WORM

ALSO BY CHRISTOPHER PAOLINI

The Inheritance Cycle:

Eragon

Eldest

Brisingr

Inheritance

CHRISTOPHER PAOLINI

THE FORK, THE WITCH, AND THE WORM

Tales from Alagaësia

○○○

VOLUME 1: ERAGON

with **ANGELA PAOLINI**
*writing as Angela the Herbalist in
"On the Nature of Stars"*

PENGUIN BOOKS

As always, this is for my family.
And also for the readers who made this possible.

PENGUIN BOOKS

UK | USA | Canada | Ireland | Australia
India | New Zealand | South Africa

Penguin Books is part of the Penguin Random House group of companies
whose addresses can be found at global.penguinrandomhouse.com.

www.penguin.co.uk   www.puffin.co.uk   www.ladybird.co.uk

Penguin
Random House
UK

First published in the USA by Alfred A. Knopf, an imprint of Random House
Children's Books, a division of Penguin Random House LLC, 2018
Published in Great Britain by Penguin Books 2019

001

Text copyright © Christopher Paolini, 2018
Inside illustrations copyright © Christopher Paolini, 2018
Eragon text copyright © Christopher Paolini, 2002
Jacket art copyright © John Jude Palencar, 2018

Map colourization by Immanuela Meijer

The moral right of the author and illustrator has been asserted

Printed and bound in Great Britain by Clays Ltd, Elcograf S.p.A.

A CIP catalogue record for this book is available from the British Library

HARDBACK
ISBN: 978–0–241–39236–2

INTERNATIONAL PAPERBACK
ISBN: 978–0–241–39237–9

All correspondence to:
Penguin Books
Penguin Random House Children's
80 Strand, London WC2R 0RL

MIX
Paper from
responsible sources
FSC® C018179

Penguin Random House is committed to a
sustainable future for our business, our readers
and our planet. This book is made from Forest
Stewardship Council® certified paper.

Contents

PART ONE: THE FORK

I. Mount Arngor   3

II. A Fork in the Road   24

III. The Hall of Colors   75

PART TWO: THE WITCH

IV. Rhymes and Riddles   83

V. On the Nature of Stars   95

VI. Questions and Answers   120

PART THREE: THE WORM

VII. Deadfall   129

VIII. The Worm of Kulkaras   147

IX. New Beginnings   260

Names and Languages   267

Afterword   275

PART ONE

The Fork

CHAPTER I

Mount Arngor

The day had not gone well.

Eragon leaned back in his chair and took a long drink of blackberry mead from the mug by his hand. Sweet warmth blossomed in his throat, and with it memories of summer afternoons spent picking berries in Palancar Valley.

A pang of homesickness struck him.

The mead had been the best thing to come out of his meeting with Hruthmund, the dwarven representative. A gift to strengthen the bonds of friendly association between dwarves and Riders—or so Hruthmund had claimed.

Eragon snorted. *Some friendship.* He'd spent the whole meeting arguing with Hruthmund over when the dwarves would deliver the supplies they'd promised. Hruthmund seemed to believe once every three to four months was more than sufficient, which was absurd considering the dwarves lived closer to the Academy than any of the other races. Even Nasuada had managed to send monthly shipments from the other side of the Hadarac Desert, far to the west.

I'll have to arrange a talk with Orik and sort it out with him directly. Just one more thing to do amid a seemingly endless sea of tasks.

Eragon eyed the mounds of scrolls, books, maps, and loose pieces of parchment that covered the desk in front of him, all of which required his attention. He sighed, finding the sight depressing.

He shifted his gaze out the large, rough-hewn windows that fronted the eyrie. Rays of evening light streamed across the windswept plains that lay below, surrounding Mount Arngor. To the north and west, the Edda River gleamed like a ribbon of beaten silver draped across the landscape. A pair of ships lay docked along the nearest bend, and from that docking, a trail led south to the foothills piled about the base of Arngor.

The mountain had been Eragon's choice—in consultation with Saphira and their traveling companions—for the Dragon Riders' new home. It was more than that too: a safeguard for the Eldunarí and, hopefully, a nesting ground for the next generation of dragons.

The high, slab-sided peak was a trailing remnant of the Beor Mountains, shorter than those towering giants but still many times bigger than the mountains of the Spine Eragon had grown up with. It stood alone in the green expanse of the eastern reaches, two weeks of slow sailing beyond the bounds of Alagaësia proper.

South of Arngor the land was rumpled like a blanket and ruffled with trees whose leaves shone silver in the wind, bright as the scales of a fish. Farther to the east stood scarps and cliffs and huge, flat-topped pillars of stone crested with piles of vegetation. Among them lived groups of wandering tribes: strange, half-wild humans the likes of which Eragon had never encountered before. So far they had proven no trouble, but he remained wary.

Such was his responsibility now.

The mountain bore many names. Arngor was Dwarvish for *White Mountain*, and indeed, the upper thirds were clad in snow and ice and—from a distance—the peak glowed with a startling brilliance amid the verdant plains. But it also had an older, secret name in Dwarvish. For as the expedition Eragon led had begun to settle among the foothills of the mountain, they had discovered tunnels burrowed into the stone beneath, and there in runes inscribed *Gor Narrveln*, which meant *Mountain of Gems*. Some ancient clan or tribe of dwarves had sunk mines deep into the roots of the peak.

The dwarves who had joined Eragon's group had been excited by the discovery, and they spent much time debating who had made the mines and what gems might still be found.

In the ancient language, the mountain was known as Fell Thindarë, which meant *Mountain of Night*. The elves could not tell Eragon where the name came from—nor the reason for it—so he rarely used it. But he also heard them refer to the peak as Vaeta, or *Hope*. He found this fitting, as the Dragon Riders were a hope for all the races of Alagaësia.

The Urgals had their own name for the peak: Ungvek. When Eragon asked them what it meant, they claimed it was *Strong-Headed*. But he wasn't so sure.

Then too there were the humans. Eragon had heard them use all of the names interchangeably, as well as refer to the mountain as Hoarspike, a term he suspected the traders often used in jest.

Personally, Eragon preferred the sound of *Arngor*, but he gave each of the names the respect they were due. The confusion surrounding them embodied the situation at the Academy: the place was a mix of races and cultures and conflicting agendas, and all of them still unsettled. . . .

He took another sip of the Mûnnvlorss mead; that was how Hruthmund had named the bottle. *Mûnnvlorss*. Eragon turned the name over on his tongue, feeling the shape of it as he attempted to pick out the meaning.

There had been other problems throughout the day, not just the meeting with Hruthmund. The Urgals had been belligerent as always. The

humans fractious. The dragons in their Eldunarí
enigmatic. And the elves . . . the elves were el-
egant and efficient and polite to a fault, but once
they made a decision, they would not or *could
not* change their minds. Dealing with them had
proven far more frustrating than Eragon had anticipated, and the more time he spent around
them, the more he'd begun to agree with Orik's
opinion of elves. They were best admired from a
distance.

In addition to the interpersonal difficulties,
there were also ongoing concerns regarding the
construction of the stronghold, the acquisition of
food and other provisions for the upcoming winter, and the myriad of other details that attended
the governance of a large town.

Which was, in essence, what their expedition
had become. A settlement, soon to be a permanent one.

Eragon drained the last of the mead. He could

feel a faint tilt to the floor underneath him as it took effect. Half the morning he'd spent devoting himself to assisting in the actual construction of the hold, and it had consumed far more of his strength and Saphira's than he'd anticipated. No matter how much he ate, it never seemed enough to replace the energy expended. In the last two weeks, he'd lost a matching two notches on his belt, and that was on top of the notch he'd taken in over the prior weeks.

He scowled as he eyed the parchment on the desk.

Restoring the race of dragons, leading the Riders, and protecting the Eldunarí were all responsibilities he wanted, welcomed, and took seriously. And yet . . . Eragon had never expected that he would spend so much of his life doing *this*. Sitting at a desk laboring over facts and figures until his vision blurred from the strain. As ridiculously stressful as fighting the Empire and facing Galbatorix had been—and Eragon never, *ever* wanted to experience anything similar—it had been exciting too.

At times he dreamed of strapping on his sword, Brisingr, getting on Saphira, and setting out to see what adventure they could find. It was just that, though: a dream. They couldn't leave the dragons or the Riders to fend for themselves, not for a long while yet.

"Barzûl," Eragon muttered. His scowl deepened as he considered a whole host of curses he could cast on the scraps of parchment: fire, frost, lightning, wind, obliteration by disintegration, and more besides.

He let out his breath, straightened up, and again reached for a quill.

Stop, said Saphira. Across the chamber, she stirred in the padded hollow that was sunk into the floor: a nest big enough for a dragon. The same nest where, each night, he slept curled up beneath one of her wings.

As she rose, flecks of blue refracted from her gemlike scales and spun across the walls in a dazzling display.

"I can't," Eragon said. "I wish I could, but I can't. These manifests have to be checked by morning, and—"

Always there will be work, she said, walking over to the desk. The tips of her gleaming claws tapped against the stone. *Always there will be those who need something of us, but you have to take care of yourself, little one. You've done enough for the day. Put aside your pen and let go of your worries. There is still light in the sky. Go spar with Blödhgarm or butt heads with Skarghaz or do something other than sit and smolder.*

"No," said Eragon, fixing his gaze on the rows of runes covering the parchment. "It has to be done, and there isn't anyone else who can do it but me. If I don't—"

He jumped as Saphira's left foreclaw stabbed

through the pile of parchment, pinning it to
the desk and spilling the bottle of ink across the
floor.

Enough, she said. She whuffed, blowing her hot
breath over him. Then she extended her neck and
peered at him with one of her glittering, bottom-
less eyes. *No more for today. You are not yourself at
the moment. Go.*

"You can't—"

Go! Her lip curled, and a deep rumble emanated from within her chest.

Eragon bit back his words, frustrated. Then
he tossed the quill next to her claw. "Fine." He
pushed the chair away from the desk, stood, and
held up his hands. "Fine. You win. I'm going."

Good. A hint of amusement appeared in her
eyes, and she pushed him toward the archway with
her snout. *Go. And don't come back until you're in
a better mood.*

"Hmph."

But he smiled as he walked through the arch and started down the wide, curved ramp of stairs outside. Despite his protestations, Eragon wasn't sorry to be away from his desk. Somewhat to his annoyance, he knew Saphira was well aware of that, but it wasn't worth grouching about something so small.

Sometimes it was easier to fight a battle than to figure out how to deal with the more mundane details of life.

That was a lesson he was still learning.

The steps were shallow, but the walls between them were wide enough for Saphira to pass between with ease. Except for personal quarters, everything in the hold was being built for use by all but the very largest dragons, same as the structures on Vroengard Island—the old home of the Dragon Riders. It was a necessary feature of the hold, but it meant that building even a single room was a monumental exercise, and most of the chambers were huge and forbidding, even more so than in the great dwarf city of Tronjheim.

The hold would feel more friendly, Eragon thought, once they had the time and energy to decorate it. Some banners and tapestries hung on the walls and a few rugs before the fireplaces would go a long way toward dampening the echoes, adding color, and generally improving the overall impression of the place. So far, the only real addition had been scores of the dwarves' flameless lanterns, which had been mounted in brackets at regular intervals along the walls.

Not that there was much to the hold at the moment. A handful of storerooms; a few walls; the eyrie where he and Saphira slept, high upon a finger of rock overlooking the rest of the planned citadel. Far more needed to be built and excavated before the complex would begin to resemble anything close to what Eragon envisioned.

He wandered down to the main courtyard,

which was nothing more than a square of rough stone littered with tools, ropes, and tents. The Urgals were wrestling around their fire, as they often did, and though Eragon watched for a while, he felt no inclination to join in.

Two of the elves—Ästrith and Rílven—who were standing guard along the battlements overlooking the foothills below, nodded as he approached. Eragon returned the gesture and stood some distance away from them, his hands clasped behind his back while he scented the evening air.

Then he went to inspect the construction of the main hall. The dwarves had designed it according to his general plan, and then the elves had refined the details. *That* had occasioned more than a little argument between the two groups.

From the hall, Eragon went to the storerooms and began to catalog the crates and barrels of supplies that had arrived the previous day. Despite

Saphira's admonishments, he couldn't bring himself to let go of his work.

So *much* yet needed doing, and he never had enough time or energy to accomplish even a fraction of his goals.

In the back of his head, he could feel Saphira's faint disapproval that he wasn't out carousing with the dwarves or sparring with the elves or doing something, *anything*, other than work. Yet none of those things appealed to Eragon. He didn't feel like fighting. Didn't feel like reading. Didn't feel like devoting energy to activities that wouldn't help him resolve the problems facing them.

For it was all resting on him. Him and Saphira. Every choice they made affected not only the future of the Riders but the very survival of the dragons, and if they chose badly, both might end.

Thoughts like that made it difficult to relax.

Driven by his discontent, Eragon climbed back

up the stairs toward the eyrie. Only he turned aside before reaching the top and, through a small side tunnel, entered the chamber they'd dug out—with spells and pickaxes—directly below.

It was a large, disk-shaped chamber. In the center, upon several tiered daises, sat an assortment of glittering Eldunarí. Mostly those he and Saphira had fetched from the Vault of Souls on Vroengard, but also a few of the hearts of hearts that Galbatorix had kept slaved to his will.

The rest of the Eldunarí—those Galbatorix had driven mad with his spells and mental tortures—were kept stored in a cave deep within the side of Mount Arngor. There they could not hurt anyone with the lashings of their unhinged thoughts, and Eragon hoped, in time, he might be able to heal them with help from the other dragons. But it would be the work of years, if not decades.

Had it been up to him, he would have placed

all the Eldunarí in such caves, along with the many dragon eggs. It was the best way to protect them, the safest sort of strongbox. Eragon was acutely aware of the risk of theft, despite the many wards he'd set on the chamber.

However, Glaedr, Umaroth, and the other dragons still in full possession of their minds had refused to live underground. As Umaroth said, *We spent over a hundred years locked in the Vault of Souls. Perhaps someday we shall spend another hundred years waiting in darkness. In the meantime, we would feel the light upon our facets.*

So it was.

The larger Eldunarí rested upon the central dais, while the smaller ones had been arranged in rings about them. Piercing the circular wall of the chamber were dozens of narrow lancet windows, which the elves had fitted with pieces of crystal that split the incoming light into flecks of rainbow. No matter the time of day, the north-facing room was always bright and strewn with multi-hued shards, both from the windows and the Eldunarí themselves.

The dwarves and the elves had taken to calling the room the Hall of Colors, and Eragon was inclined to agree with the choice. It was a fitting description indeed.

He made his way to the center and knelt in front of the sparkling, gold-hued gem that was Glaedr's heart of hearts. The dragon's mind touched his own, and Eragon felt a vast vista of thought and feeling open up before him. As always, it was a humbling experience.

What troubles you, Eragon-finiarel?

Still restless, Eragon pursed his lips and looked past the Eldunarí at the semi-transparent crystal filling the windows. *Too much work. I can't get ahead of it, and because of that, I can't bring myself to do anything else. It's wearing on me.*

You must learn to center yourself, said Glaedr. *Then these lesser concerns will not bother you.*

I know. . . . And I know there are many, many things I can't control. Eragon allowed himself a brief, grim smile. *But knowing and doing are two different things.*

Then another mind joined theirs, that of Umaroth, one of the oldest Eldunarí. Out of reflex, Eragon glanced toward the white heart of hearts that contained the dragon's consciousness.

Umaroth said, *What you need is a distraction, that your mind might rest and reset.*

That I do, said Eragon.

Then perhaps we can help, Argetlam. Remember you how my wingmates and I kept watch upon Alagaësia from within the Vault of Souls?

. . . Yes, said Eragon, already having an inkling of what the dragon was hinting at.

He was right. *We have continued the practice,*

Argetlam, as a means of whiling away the days, but also that we might stay abreast of events and not be surprised by the rise of some new enemy.

More minds joined Umaroth's: the rest of the Eldunarí, pressing in around Eragon's consciousness like a sea of growling voices. As always, it took a concentrated effort to ward them off and keep hold of his own thoughts. *Why am I not surprised?*

If you wish, said Glaedr, *we can show you some of what we see. A vision of elsewhere that might provide you with a new perspective.*

Eragon hesitated as he considered the offer. *How long will it take?*

As long as is required, youngling, said Umaroth. *Worrying about the time is exactly what you need curing of. Does the eagle worry about the length of the day? Does the bear or the deer or the fish in the sea? No. So why should you? Chew what you can and leave the rest for tomorrow.*

All right, said Eragon. He lifted his chest and took a deep breath as he prepared himself. *Show me, then.*

Inexorable as the onrushing tide, the dragons' minds washed over his own. They swept Eragon out of his body, out of the Hall of Colors and away from snow-clad Mount Arngor and all his cares and worries, carrying him toward the familiar yet distant lands of Alagaësia.

Images blossomed before him, and within them Eragon saw and felt far more than he'd expected. . . .

✦ ✦ ✦

CHAPTER II

A Fork in the Road

It was two days past Maddentide, and the first flakes of snow were drifting from the starry sky onto the city of Ceunon.

Essie didn't notice. She stomped down the cobblestone alley behind the Yarstead house, her mouth set in a hard line and her cheeks burning as she struggled not to cry. She hated stupid, mean Hjordis, with her fake smile and her pretty bows and all her nasty little insults. *Hated* her.

And then there was poor Carth. Essie couldn't stop thinking about his reaction. He had looked so betrayed when she'd pushed him into the trough. He hadn't even said anything, just sat where he had fallen and gaped at her while his eyes went big and round.

Her dress sleeve was still wet from where the muddy water had splashed her.

The familiar sound of waves slapping against the underside of the wharves grew louder as she approached the docks. She kept to the alleys— kept to the narrow ways that the adults rarely used. Overhead, a rook with fluffed-out feathers sat perched on the eaves of the Sorting House. It cocked its head and opened its beak to utter a mournful cry.

Essie shivered, though not from the cold, and pulled her shawl closer around her shoulders. A dog had howled during the night, the candle on the little shelf where they left offerings of milk and bread for the Svartlings had gone out, and now a lone rook had called. Bad omens all. Was there more ill fortune coming her way? She didn't think she could bear anything worse. . . .

She slipped between the smelly drying racks by the edge of the fish market and came into the street. Ahead of her, music and conversation sounded, and warm light spilled out of the front of the Fulsome Feast. The windows of the inn were crystal, specially made by the dwarves, and they gleamed like diamond in the flickering light. It was a point of pride for Essie every time she saw the windows, even now. No other building on the street had anything so pretty.

Inside, the common room was as loud and busy as ever. Essie ignored the guests and went to the bar. Papa was there pouring beer, washing out mugs, and serving dishes of smoked herring. He glanced at her as she ducked under the half door at the end of the bar.

"You're late," he said.

"Sorry, Papa." Essie got a plate and loaded it with

a heel of bread, a wedge of hard Sartos cheese, and a half-dried apple—all taken from the shelf under the bar. She was still too small to help with the serving, but she would help with the cleaning up later.

And then later still, once everyone had gone to bed, she would sneak down to the cellar, gather the supplies she needed. . . .

She carried the plate to an empty chair in front of the great stone fireplace. Next to the chair was a small table, and on the other side of it, a second chair—this one with a man sitting in it. He was lean and dark-eyed, with a neat beard and a long black travel cloak bunched around him. A plate balanced on his knee, and he was slowly eating a serving of Mama's roasted turnips and mutton, stabbing at the pieces with one of the inn's iron forks.

Essie didn't care. He was just another traveler, like so many who came to the Fulsome Feast.

She plopped down in the free chair and tore off part of the heel of bread, imagining that it was

Hjordis's head she was tearing off. . . . She continued to rip at the food with her fingers and teeth, and
she chewed with a ferocity that was oddly satisfying.

She still felt as if she was about to cry, which
just made her more angry. Crying was for little
children. Crying was for weaklings who got pushed
around and told what to do. That wasn't her!

She made a noise of frustration as she bit into
the apple and the stem got stuck in the gap between her front teeth.

"You seem upset," the man next to her said in
a mild tone.

Essie scowled. She plucked the stem from between her teeth and flung it into the fireplace. "It's
all Hjordis's fault!" Papa didn't like her talking to
the guests too much, but she had never minded
him. The visitors always had interesting stories,
and many of them would ruffle her hair and comment on how adorable she was and give her candied
nuts or syrup twists (in the winter, at least).

"Oh?" said the man. He put down his fork and turned in his seat to better look at her. "And who is this Hjordis?"

"She's the daughter of Jarek. He's the earl's chief mason," said Essie, sullen.

"I see. Does that make her important?"

Essie shook her head. "It makes her *think* she's important."

"What did she do to upset you, then?"

"Everything!" Essie took a savage bite out of the apple and chewed so hard and quick she bit the inside of her mouth. She winced and swallowed, trying to ignore the pain.

The man drank from the mug by his hand. "Most interesting," he said, and used a napkin to dab a fleck of foam off his mustache. "Well then, is it a tale you feel like telling? Perhaps talking about it will make you feel better."

Essie looked at him, slightly suspicious. He had an open face, but there was an intensity to his dark eyes, and a slight hardness too, that she wasn't sure about. "Papa wouldn't want me to bother you."

"I have some time," said the man easily. "I'm just waiting for a certain associate of mine who, alas, happens to be habitually late. If you wish to share your tale of woe, then please, consider me your devoted audience."

He used a lot of big words, and his accent wasn't one Essie was familiar with. It seemed overly careful, as if he were sculpting the air with his tongue. Despite that, and despite the hardness of his eyes, she decided he seemed like a nice person.

She bounced her feet off the legs of the chair. "Well . . . I'd like to tell you, but I can't possibly unless we're friends."

"Is that so? And how do we become friends?"

"You have to tell me your name! Silly."

The man smiled. He had pretty teeth. "Of course. How foolish of me. In that case, my name is Tornac." And he held out his hand. His fingers were long and pale, but strong-looking. His nails were trimmed square.

"Essie Siglingsdaughter." She could feel a row of calluses on his palm as they shook hands.

"Very nice to meet you, Essie. Now then, what seems to be bothering you?"

Essie stared at the partially eaten apple in her hand. She sighed and put it back on the plate. "It's all Hjordis's fault."

"So you said."

"She's always being mean to me and making her friends tease me."

Tornac's expression grew serious. "That's not good at all."

Encouraged, Essie shook her head, allowing her outrage to shine forth. "No! I mean . . . sometimes they tease me anyway, but, um, Hjordis—when she's there, it gets really bad."

"Is that what happened today?"

"Yes. Sort of." She broke off a piece of cheese

and nibbled on it while she thought back over the past few weeks. Tornac waited patiently. She liked that about him. He reminded her of a cat. Finally, she gathered the courage to say, "Before harvest, Hjordis started being nicer to me. I thought— I thought maybe things were going to be better. She even invited me to her house." Essie glanced at Tornac. "It's right by the castle."

"Impressive."

Essie nodded, glad he understood. "She gave me one of her ribbons, a yellow one, and said that I could come to her Maddentide party."

"And did you?"

Another bob of her head. "It—it was today." Hot tears filled her eyes, and she blinked furiously, disappointed with herself.

"Here now," said Tornac, looking concerned. He held out a square of soft white cloth.

At first Essie was reluctant to accept. The cloth was so clean! But then the tears started running down her cheeks, and she grabbed the kerchief and wiped her eyes. "Thank you, mister."

Another small smile appeared on the man's face. "It's been a long time since I've been called *mister*, but you're very welcome. I take it the party didn't go well?"

Essie scowled and pushed the kerchief back toward him. She *wasn't* going to cry anymore. Not her. "The party was fine. It was Hjordis. She got mean again, after, and . . . and"—Essie took a deep breath, as if to fill her stomach with courage—"and she said that if I didn't do what she wanted, she would tell her father not to use our inn during the solstice celebration." She peered at Tornac, wondering if he knew why that was so important. "All the masons come here to drink and"—she hiccupped, despite herself—"they drink a lot, and it means they spend stacks and stacks of coppers."

Tornac put his plate on the table and leaned toward her. His cloak rustled like wind in the thatching. His face was very serious. "What did she want you to do?"

Ashamed, Essie stared at her muddy shoes. "She wanted me to push Carth into a horse trough," she said, tripping over the words in her rush to get them out.

"Carth is a friend of yours?"

Essie nodded, miserable. They'd known each other since she was three. "He lives on the docks. His father is a fisher."

"So he wouldn't get invited to a party like this."

"No, but Hjordis sent her handmaid to bring him to the house and . . ." Essie stared at Tornac, her expression fierce. "I didn't have no choice! If I hadn't pushed him, then she would have told her father not to come to the Fulsome Feast."

"I understand," said Tornac in a soothing tone. "So you pushed your friend. Were you able to apologize to him?"

"No," Essie said, feeling even worse. "I—I ran.

But everyone saw. He won't want to be friends with me anymore. No one will. Hjordis just meant to trick me, and I *hate* her." Essie grabbed the apple and took another quick bite. Her teeth clacked together.

Tornac opened his mouth to say something, but at that moment, Papa came by on his way to deliver a pair of mugs to a table by the wall. He gave her a disapproving look. "My daughter isn't making a nuisance of herself, is she, Master Tornac? She has a bad habit of pestering guests when they're trying to eat."

"Not at all," said Tornac, smiling. "I've been on the road for far too long with nothing but the sun and the moon for company. A bit of conversation is exactly what I need. In fact—" His fingers dipped under his belt, and Essie saw a flash of silver as he reached out to her father. "Perhaps you can see to it that the tables next to us remain clear. I'm expecting an associate of mine, and we have some, ah, business to discuss."

The coins disappeared into his apron, and Papa bobbed his head. "Of course, Master Tornac." He glanced at her again, his expression slightly concerned, and then continued on his way.

Essie felt a sudden pang of remorse. Papa was going to be so sad when she was gone. But there was no other choice. She *had* to leave.

"Now then," said Tornac, stretching his long legs out toward the fire. "You were telling me your tale of woe, Essie Siglingsdaughter. Was that the full accounting?"

"That was it," Essie said in a small voice.

Tornac picked up the fork from his plate and began to twirl it between his fingers. She found the sight vaguely entrancing. "Things can't be as bad as you think. I'm sure if you explain to your friend—"

"No," she said, firm. She knew Carth. He wouldn't forgive her for what she'd done. None of her friends along the docks would. They'd think she'd turned against them to join Hjordis and the other children by the castle. And in a way, she had. "He won't understand. He won't trust me again. They'll hate me for it."

A cutting edge entered Tornac's voice. "Then maybe they weren't really your friends."

Essie couldn't bear the thought. "They were. You don't understand!" And she brought her fist down on the arm of the chair in an impatient stamp. "Carth is . . . He's really nice. Everyone likes him, and now they won't like me. You wouldn't know. You're all big and . . . and old."

Tornac's eyebrows climbed toward his hairline. "You might be surprised what I know. So they won't like you. What are you going to do about it?"

Essie didn't mean to say, but the words slipped out of her before she thought better of it: "I'm going to run away." The moment she realized what she'd done, she gave Tornac a panicked look. "Don't tell Papa, please!"

Tornac took another sip from his mug and

then smoothed his beard. He didn't seem upset by her plan, not the way Essie knew Papa would be. Rather, he seemed to be taking her seriously, which Essie liked.

"And where would you go?" he asked.

Essie had already been thinking about that. "South, where it's warm. There's a caravan leaving tomorrow. The foreman comes here. He's nice. I can sneak out, and then ride with them to Gil'ead."

Tornac picked at his fork with the tip of a fingernail. "And then?"

After that, things got a bit hazy in Essie's mind, but she knew what her ultimate goal would be. "I want to visit the Beor Mountains and see the dwarves!" she said. The thought excited her. "They made our windows. Aren't they pretty?" She pointed.

"They certainly are," said Tornac.

"Have you ever visited the Beor Mountains?"

"I have," said Tornac. "Once, long ago."

Impressed, Essie looked at him with renewed interest. "Really? Are they as tall as everyone says?"

"So tall the peaks aren't even visible."

She leaned back in her chair as she tried to picture that. The effort made her dizzy. "How wonderful."

A snort escaped Tornac. "If you don't count being shot at with arrows, then yes. . . . You do realize, Essie Siglingsdaughter, that running away won't solve your problems here."

"Of course not," she said. His statement seemed very obvious to her. "But if I leave, then Hjordis can't bother me anymore." Essie made a face.

Tornac almost looked as if he were going to laugh, but then he took another sip from his mug, and afterward he seemed more solemn. "Or, and this is just a suggestion, you could try to fix the problem instead of running away."

"It can't be fixed," she said, stubborn.

"What about your parents? I'm sure they would miss you terribly. Do you really want to make them suffer like that?"

Essie crossed her arms. This wasn't going the way she wanted. Tornac had been agreeable so far. Why was he arguing with her now? "They have my brother and my sister and Olfa. He's only two." She pouted. "They wouldn't miss me."

"I very much doubt that," said Tornac. "Besides, think what you did with Hjordis. You helped protect the Fulsome Feast. If your parents understood the sacrifice you made, I'm sure they would be very proud."

"Uh-huh," said Essie, unconvinced. "There wouldn't have been a problem if it wasn't for me. *I'm* the problem. If I go away, everything will be all right." Feeling determined, she picked up the apple core and threw it into the great fireplace.

A whirl of sparks flew up the chimney, and she heard the sizzle of water exploding into steam.

In an overly casual tone, Tornac said, "What is that?"

"What?" she said.

"There, on your arm."

Essie looked down and saw her sleeve had ridden up, exposing the twisted red scar on her left wrist. Ashamed, she tugged the cuff down. "Nothing," she mumbled.

"May I?" said Tornac, and held out his hand toward her. At first Essie hesitated, but he seemed so polite and so assured that at last she relented and let him take her arm.

As gently as her mother would, Tornac pulled back the cuff of her sleeve. Essie turned her head away. She didn't need to see the scar again—didn't need to look to know how it crawled up her forearm all the way to her elbow.

She hoped no one else in the common room would notice.

After a moment, she felt Tornac pull her

sleeve back down, and he said, "That . . . is a very impressive scar. You should be proud of it."

Confused, she looked back at him. "Why? It's ugly, and I hate it."

A faint smile played around the corners of his lips. "Because a scar means you survived. It means you're tough and hard to kill. It means you *lived*. A scar is something to admire."

"You're wrong," said Essie. She pointed at the pot with the painted bluebells on the mantel—the one Auntie Helna had given them last winter, the one Essie had knocked onto the floor a few moons back. A long crack ran from the lip of the pot to the base. "It just means you're broken."

"Ah," said Tornac in a soft voice. "But sometimes, if you work very hard, you can mend a break so that it's stronger than before."

Essie wasn't liking their conversation as much as she had earlier. She crossed her arms, tucking her left hand into her armpit. "Hjordis and the others always make fun of me for it," she mumbled. "They say my arm is as red as a snapper, and that I'll never get a husband because of it."

"And what do your parents say?"

Essie made a face. "That it doesn't matter. But that's not true, is it?"

Tornac inclined his head. "No. I suppose it isn't. Your parents are doing their best to protect you, though."

"Well, they can't," she said, and huffed. She glanced at him; the darkness had returned to his face, but it didn't seem to be directed at her. "Do you have any scars?" she asked.

A humorless laugh escaped him. "Oh yes." He pointed at a small white mark on his chin. "This one is only a few months old. A friend of mine gave it to me by accident while we were playing around, the big oaf." A hint of affection lightened Tornac's expression. Then he said, "What happened to your arm?"

It took Essie a while to answer. All she could see in her head was the inn's kitchen that morning three years ago, and all she could hear were Mama's frantic cries. . . . "It was an accident," she mumbled. "A pot with hot water fell onto my arm."

Tornac's eyes narrowed. "It just *fell* on you?"

Essie nodded. She didn't want to mention that it had been Papa who bumped her. But it hadn't been his fault! She'd been running around the kitchen, and he hadn't seen her, and Essie knew he felt terrible about what had happened.

"Mmm." Tornac was staring at the fire, the sparks and embers reflecting in his eyes.

Essie looked at him, curious. "Where are you from?" she asked.

"A long, long way from here."

"In the south?"

"Yes, in the south."

She kicked her feet against the chair. "What's

it like there?" If she was going to run away, she ought to know what to expect.

Tornac inhaled slowly and tilted his head back so he was gazing at the ceiling. "It depends where you go. There are hot places and cold places, and places where the wind never stops blowing. Forests seemingly without end. Caves that burrow into the deepest parts of the earth, and plains full of vast herds of red deer."

"Are there monsters?" she asked.

"Of course," he said, returning his gaze to her. "There are always monsters. Some of them even look like humans. . . . I ran away from home myself, you know."

"You did?"

He nodded. "I was older than you, but yes. I ran, but I didn't escape what I was running from. . . . Listen to me, Essie. I know you think leaving will make everything better, but—"

"There you are, Tornac of the Road," said a sly,

slithering voice that made the hair on the back of Essie's neck prickle. A man stepped forward between the tables. He was thin and stooped, with a patched cloak draped over his shoulders and ragged clothes underneath. Rings glittered on his fingers.

Essie took an instant dislike to the man. He smelled of wet fur, and something about the way he moved and looked gave her a warning feeling in her gut.

"Sarros," said Tornac, a flicker of distaste on his face. "I've been waiting for you."

"The reaches are dangerous these days," said Sarros. He picked up an empty chair and placed it between Essie and Tornac, and then sat facing both of them.

Essie noticed several more men had entered the common room from the street. Six of them. They were rough-looking, but not like the fishermen; they wore furs and leathers and had a wild appearance similar to the trappers who came in during spring. Papa often had to throw them out because they made too much trouble.

Over by the bar, Papa watched the new-comers, wary. He pulled out his leather-wrapped truncheon and laid it next to his washcloth as a silent warning. The sight comforted Essie; she had seen him settle even the meanest drunks with a few well-placed blows.

Sarros pointed at her with one long, grimy forefinger. "We have business to discuss. Send the youngling away."

"I have nothing to hide," said Tornac smoothly. "She can stay." He glanced at her. "If you're in-terested. You might learn something useful of the world by it."

Essie shrank back in her seat, but she didn't leave. Tornac's words tickled her curiosity. Also, for some reason, she couldn't help but remember the bad omens from earlier, and she felt that if she did leave, something horrible would happen to Tornac.

A long hiss sounded between Sarros's teeth as he shook his head. "Foolish, Wanderer. Do as you wish, then. I'll not argue, even if you put your foot crosswise."

A glint of steel appeared in Tornac's gaze. "No, you won't. Tell me, then, what have you found? It's been three months, and—"

Sarros waved a hand. "Yes, yes. Three months. I told you; the reaches are dangerous. But I found word of what you seek. Better than word, I found *this*—" From the leather wallet on his belt, he produced a fist-sized chunk of black *something* that he thumped down on the table.

Essie leaned forward, as did Tornac.

The something was a piece of rock, but there was a deep shine to it unlike any rock Essie had seen, as if a smoldering coal were buried in the center. She sniffed and then wrinkled her nose. Yuck! It smelled as bad as a rotten egg.

Tornac looked at the rock as if he wasn't sure he believed it existed. "What exactly is that?"

Sarros lifted his shoulders, shrugging like the herons along the docks. "Suspicions of shadows are all I have, but you sought the unusual, the out-of-place, and that there doesn't fit in the normal frame."

"Were there more, or . . . ?"

Sarros nodded. "I am told. A whole field scattered with stones."

"Black and burnt?"

"As if seared by fire, but with no sign of flame or smoke."

Essie said, "Where is it from?"

Sarros smiled unpleasantly. His teeth, she noticed, had been sharpened to points. The sight disgusted her more than it frightened her. "Well now, that there is the nub of it, youngling. Yes indeed."

Tornac reached for the rock, and Sarros dropped

a hand over the shiny chunk, caging it behind his fingers. "No," he said. "Coin first, Wanderer."

Tornac pressed his lips together and then produced a small leather pouch from under his heavy cloak. The clink of metal sounded as he put it on the table.

Sarros's smile widened. He tugged loose the pouch's drawstring, and Essie glimpsed a yellow gleam inside. She took a sharp breath. *Gold!* She'd never even seen a whole crown before.

"Half now," said Tornac. "And the rest when you tell me where you found that." He poked the rock with the tip of a finger.

A strange choking sound came from Sarros. It took Essie a second to realize that the man was laughing. Then he said, "Oh no, Wanderer. No indeed. I think instead you should give us the rest of your coin, and perhaps then we'll let you keep your head."

Across the common room, the fur-clad men

slipped hands under their cloaks, and Essie saw the hilts of swords, half hidden beneath.

She stiffened and, panicked, looked to her father. A guest had distracted him: one of the laborers from the docks stood leaning against the bar, chattering away. She opened her mouth and was about to cry out a warning when Sarros drew a thin-bladed knife and pressed it against her throat.

"Ah-ah," he said. "Not a peep from you, youngling, or I'll open your throat from stem to stern."

Fear froze Essie in place. She could barely breathe, she was so scared of the razor edge touching her skin, cold and deadly. Suddenly all of her previous worries didn't seem important in the slightest. Papa could save her—she felt sure he could—but only if he knew she was in trouble. She kept glancing toward the bar, hoping Papa would somehow sense her thoughts.

The hardness in Tornac's eyes grew even more flinty, but otherwise he remained as calm as ever.

"Why the turn of face, Sarros? I'm paying you good money."

"Yesss. That's the point." Sarros leaned in closer, lips pulled wide. His breath stank of rotting meat. "If you are willing to pay thiswise-much for hints and rumors, then you must have more coin than sense. *Much* more coin."

Essie considered kicking him in the shin, but she was too scared of the knife to try.

A frown formed on Tornac's brow, and she heard him mutter a bad word under his breath. Then he said, "This isn't a fight you want. Tell me the location, take the gold you're owed, and no one has to get hurt."

"What fight?" said Sarros, and cackled. "You have no sword on you. We are six, and you are one. The coin is ours whether you wish it or not." Essie stiffened as the steel bit into her neck, a bright little slice of pain. "See?" said Sarros. "I make the choice easy for you, Wanderer. Hand over the rest of your gold, or the youngling here will pay with blood."

Essie held her breath as she watched Tornac. Part of her expected him to pull out a hidden dagger and do something dangerous and heroic. He seemed like that kind of person. Part of her hoped he would rescue her.

Instead, all Tornac did was utter a sentence of strange words.

The air in front of him seemed to shiver, but nothing else happened. Essie didn't know what he was trying to do, but it wasn't helping.

Sarros chuckled again. "Foolish. Very foolish." With his free hand, he pulled out a bird-skull amulet from under his jerkin. "Do you see this, Wanderer? The witch-woman Bachel charmed a necklace for each of us. Your weirding ways won't help you now. We're protected against all evilness."

"Is that so?" said Tornac. And then he spoke a Word, and such a word it was. It rang like a bell, and in the sound, Essie thought she heard all possible meanings, and yet when she tried to recall the Word itself, no memory of it remained.

A dull silence followed. Everyone in the common room looked at Tornac, many of the guests with a dazed expression, as if they'd just woken from a dream.

Magic! Essie stared wide-eyed, so amazed she nearly forgot her fear. No one was supposed to use magic these days, not unless they had the approval of the queen's spellcasters, the Du Vrangr Gata. But Essie had always wanted to see the sort of magic the old stories talked about.

Despite the ringing Word, Sarros appeared unharmed, and for the first time, Tornac seemed perturbed.

"Essie!" said Papa. He grabbed his truncheon and sprang over the bar. "You let her go now!" Before he could take more than a step, two of the fur-clad men charged him and knocked him to the floor. A dull *thunk* sounded as one of them struck Papa on the head with the pommel of a sword.

He moaned and dropped the truncheon.

No one else dared move.

"Papa!" Essie cried. If not for the knife at her throat, she would have rushed to his side. She'd never seen her father lose a fight before, and the sight of him on the floor removed any last sense of safety.

Again, Sarros chuckled, louder than before. "Your tricks will not help you, Wanderer. No enchantments are as strong as Bachel's. No magic is deeper."

"Perhaps you're right," said Tornac. He seemed calm again, which Essie couldn't understand. He picked up the fork and began to fiddle with it. "Well then. It appears I have no choice in the matter."

"None whatsoever," said Sarros, smug.

Mama appeared in the doorway to the kitchen, wiping her hands on her apron. "What is all this—" she started to say, and then saw Sarros holding the knife and Papa lying on the floor, and her face went pale.

"Don't cause no trouble, or your man gets stuck," said one of the fur-clad ruffians, pointing his blade at Papa.

While everyone else was distracted by Mama, Essie saw Tornac's lips twitch as he spoke without voice, and a flame-like ripple ran the length of the fork.

If she'd blinked, she would have missed it.

Sarros slapped the table. "Enough with the yapping. Your coin, now."

Tornac tipped his head and—with his left hand—again reached under his cloak. One moment he was sitting, seemingly relaxed. Then he moved faster than Essie could follow. His cloak swung through the air, sending a rush of wind into her face, and his fork flashed across the table, and she heard a *ting!* as it knocked the knife free of

Sarros's grip and sent the weapon flying into the log wall.

Tornac sat with his arm extended, holding the tines of the fork against the underside of Sarros's chin, tickling him with the points. The sharp-toothed man swallowed. A sheen of sweat had broken out on his face.

Essie still didn't dare move; Sarros's hand was next to her neck, fingers spread wide as if to tear out her throat.

"Then again," said Tornac, "there's nothing in your charm to stop me from using magic on something else. Like this fork, for example." A feral gleam appeared in his eyes as he pressed the tines deeper into Sarros's flesh. "Do you really think I need a sword to defeat you, you tumorous sack of filth?"

Sarros hissed. Then he shoved Essie into Tornac's lap and sprang backward, knocking his chair over.

Essie fell to the floor. Terrified, she scrambled

on hands and feet between the tables until she reached Mama's side. Around her, the common room erupted into a commotion, with shouts and crashes and breaking mugs.

Her mother didn't say anything, just pulled Essie behind her skirts and grabbed a chair, which she held out in front of them, like a weapon or a shield.

The room had become a sea of thrashing bodies as the guests struggled to escape. The six fur-clad men had drawn their blades and were attempting to box in Tornac by the fireplace, but Tornac was having none of that. He had thrown off his cloak and was moving about the room, like a prowling cat. Sarros had retreated to a corner and was shouting, "Slice him crosswise! Kill him! Cut open his belly and spill his guts."

The nearest swordsman charged Tornac, swinging his blade. Tornac knocked the blow aside with his fork, and then he darted forward and buried the fork in the man's chest.

Essie had seen plenty end-of-harvest brawls, but this was nothing like a drunken fight between laborers. It was far worse: sober men trying to kill each other in open combat, and it frightened her many times more because of it.

She looked for her father and spotted him crawling toward the cover of the bar, blood dripping from a cut on his temple. "Papa!" she cried, but he didn't hear.

Three more of Sarros's men attacked Tornac. All three jabbed and slashed with their swords, not waiting for the others to take their turn.

Tornac grabbed a chair and, one-handed, smashed it over the man to his left. At the same time, he used the fork to parry the attacks from the other two brutes. He matched each of their blows, fencing with amazing skill as they tried to get past his guard. The men had the advantage of reach with their swords, but Tornac sidestepped their blades and slipped into striking range. His hand was a blur as he stabbed with the fork: one, two, three, four hard impacts that dropped the men to the floor, where they lay groaning.

Across the room, Papa reached the bar and pulled himself to his feet. He still held the truncheon in his hand, but the leather-wrapped stick seemed useless compared to the flashing swords.

"Essie," said Mama, her voice tight. "Olfa is in the kitchen. I want you to go—"

Before she could finish, one of Sarros's guards ran up to them. In his off hand, he held a mace, which he swung at the chair Mama was holding.

The impact knocked the chair out of Mama's hands, breaking it.

Essie had never felt so small or helpless as she did in that moment. Papa was too far away to help, and there was nothing Mama could do to stop the fur-clad man as he drew back the sword in his other hand—

Thud.

The man's eyes rolled until they showed white, and then he collapsed, and Essie saw the fork sticking out from the back of his head.

Tornac had thrown it from across the common room.

Sarros and his last remaining companion attempted to flank the now-weaponless Tornac. Before they could get close, Tornac kicked a table into the swordsman's stomach and—when he stumbled—jumped on him and knocked his head against the floor.

Sarros cursed and fled toward the door. As he turned, he threw a handful of glittering crystals at Tornac.

Again, Tornac spoke a Word, and at his command, the crystals swerved in midair and flew into the flames of the fire. A series of loud *pops!* sounded, and a fountain of embers sprayed the stone hearth.

Before Sarros could reach the door, Tornac

caught up with him. He grabbed the back of Sarros's jerkin and—in a stunning display of strength—lifted Sarros off the floor and over his head, and then slammed him back down onto the wooden boards.

Sarros let out a bellow of pain and clutched at his left elbow, which was bent at an unnatural angle.

"Essie," said Mama. "Stay behind me."

Essie had no intention of doing otherwise.

The few remaining guests edged away from Tornac as he planted a foot on Sarros's chest. "Now then, you bastard," he growled. "Where did you find that stone?"

Papa left the bar and staggered across the room to where Mama and Essie stood. They didn't say anything, but Mama put an arm around Papa, and he did the same to her.

A burbling laugh escaped Sarros. There was a wild note to his voice that reminded Essie of

Waeric, the madman who lived under the bridge by the mill. Sarros licked his sharpened teeth and said, "You do not know what you seek, Wanderer. You're moon-addled and nose-blind. The sleeper stirs, and you and me—we're all ants waiting to be crushed."

"The *stone*," said Tornac between clenched teeth. "Where?"

Sarros's voice grew even higher, a mad shriek that pierced the night air. "You don't understand. The Dreamers! The Dreamers! They get inside your head, and they twist your thoughts. Ahh! They twist them all out of joint." He started to thrash, drumming his heels against the floor. Yellow foam bubbled at the corners of his mouth. "They'll come for you, Wanderer, and then you'll see. They'll . . ." His voice trailed off into a hoarse croak, and then with one final jerk, he fell still.

For a moment, no one in the common room stirred.

All eyes remained on Tornac as he yanked the

amulet off Sarros's neck, retrieved his cloak, and walked back to the table by the fire. He pocketed the stone with the inner shine, picked up his pouch of coins, and then paused, considering.

Bouncing the pouch in his hand, he came over to where Papa and Mama stood shielding Essie.

"Please . . . ," said Papa. Essie had never heard him sound so desperate, and it gave her a sickening ache in her stomach. More than anything, his fear made her realize that the world was far scarier than she had originally thought. Their home had always felt like a safe place to Essie, but no longer. Neither her father nor her mother could protect her, not in the face of swords, and certainly not against magic.

"My apologies for the trouble," said Tornac. He stank of sweat, and the front of his linen shirt was splattered with blood. Nevertheless, he seemed calm again. "Here, this should make up for the mess." He held out the pouch, and after a moment's hesitation, Papa accepted it.

Papa licked his lips. "The Watch will be here any minute. If you leave out the back . . . you can make it to the gate before they see you."

Tornac nodded. Then he knelt and yanked the fork out of the head of the ruffian lying on the nearby boards. Essie shrank back as Tornac looked straight at her. "Sometimes," he said, "you have to stand and fight. Sometimes running away isn't an option. Now do you understand?"

"Yes," Essie whispered.

Tornac shifted his attention to her parents. "One last question: Do you need the patronage of the masons' guild to keep this inn open?"

Confusion furrowed Papa's brow. "No, not if it came to such. Why?"

"That's what I thought," said Tornac. Then he presented Essie with the fork. It looked perfectly clean, without so much as a drop of blood on it. "I'm giving this to you. It has a spell on it to keep it from breaking. If Hjordis bothers you again, give her a good poke, and she'll leave you alone."

"Essie," Mama said in a low, warning voice.

But Essie had already made her decision. Tornac was right: running away wasn't always an option. That wasn't her only reason either. While their home might be safer than elsewhere, she couldn't count on her parents to ward off danger. The fight in the common room had proven that. Her only real choice was to learn how to defend herself and her family.

She took the fork. "Thank you," she said, solemn.

"All good weapons deserve a name," said Tornac. "Especially magical ones. What would you call this one?"

Essie thought for a second and then said, "Mister Stabby!"

A broad smile spread across Tornac's face, and all hints of shadow vanished from his expression. He laughed, a loud, hearty laugh. "Mister Stabby. I like it. Very apt. May Mister Stabby always bring you good fortune."

And Essie smiled as well. The world was big and scary, but now she had a magical weapon. Now she had Mister Stabby! Maybe if she did poke Hjordis, Carth would forgive her. Essie could just see the expression of outrage on Hjordis's face. . . .

Then Mama said, "Who . . . who are you, really?"

"Just another person looking for answers," said Tornac. Essie thought he was going to leave then, but instead he surprised her by putting a hand on her arm. He spoke words she didn't understand, and she felt them deep inside herself, as if he had plucked a string attached to her bones.

"Leave her be!" said Papa, and pulled her

away, but Tornac was already moving past them, his cloak spreading like a dark wing behind him. As his footsteps faded out the back, both Mama and Papa ran their hands over her head and arms, checking for injuries. "Are you hurt?" said Mama. "What did he do to you? Are—"

"I'm okay," Essie said, although she wasn't sure at all. "I, *ah!*" A burning, tingling feeling swept through her left arm, and she cried out with pain. It felt like hundreds of ants were biting her.

She tore at the cuff of her sleeve, pulled it back, and saw—

—the top of her forearm crawling with a life of its own as the long, puckered scar smoothed over and began to fade into normal, healthy skin. The scar shrank and shrank, until only a small red S-shape was left. But it didn't vanish entirely: a remembrance of past pain. Of survival.

Essie stared, hardly able to believe. She

touched the new skin, and then looked at her parents. This time, she made no effort to stop the tears that rolled down her cheeks.

"Oh, Essie," Papa said, his voice thick with emotion, and he and Mama folded her into a warm embrace.

✦ ✦ ✦

Outside the Fulsome Feast, Murtagh lifted his head and took a deep breath of the night air. Soft petals of snow fell around him, and the whole city felt still and quiet, muffled beneath a low layer of clouds.

His heart was pounding; it had yet to slow after the fight in the tavern. *Stupid.* He should have realized that spending so much gold might cause a problem. It wasn't a mistake he would make again.

How long had it been since he'd last killed a man? Over a year. A pair of bandits had jumped him as he was heading back to camp one evening—foolish, uneducated louts who hadn't the slightest chance of taking him down. He'd fought back out of reflex, and by the time he knew what was happening, the two unfortunates were already lying on the ground. He still remembered the whimpers the one kid had made as he died. . . .

Murtagh grimaced. Some people went their whole lives without killing. He wondered what that was like.

A drop of blood—not his own—trickled down the back of his hand. Disgusted, Murtagh scraped it off against the side of the building. The splinters bothered him less than the gore.

Even though he hadn't gotten a location from Sarros, at least he now knew that the place he was looking for existed. The knowledge left him feeling uneasy. He would have far preferred disappointment. Whatever truth lay hidden beneath the field of blackened earth, he doubted it would herald anything good or pleasant. Life was never so simple. And who were the Dreamers Sarros had mentioned? Always more mysteries . . .

A questioning thought reached him from outside Ceunon: Thorn worried for his safety.

I'm fine, Murtagh told him. *Just a bit of trouble.*

Do I need to come?

I don't think so, but stand by in any case.

Always.

Thorn subsided with a sense of cautious watchfulness, but Murtagh felt the ever-present thread of connection that joined them: a comforting closeness that had become the one unchanging reality in their lives.

He started through the alley. Time to go. It wouldn't be long before the city Watch arrived to investigate the disturbance in the tavern, and he'd lingered long enough.

A flicker of motion high above caught his attention.

Murtagh stopped to look. At first he wasn't sure what he was seeing.

Sailing down from the underside of the fire-lit clouds was a small ship of grass, no more than a hand or two in length. The hull and sail were made of woven blades, and the mast and spars built from lengths of stem.

No crew—if however diminutive—was to be seen; the ship moved of its own accord, driven and sustained by an invisible force. It circled him twice, and he saw a tiny pennant fluttering above the equally tiny crow's nest.

Then the ship turned westward and vanished within the veil of descending snow, leaving be-hind no trace of its existence.

Murtagh smiled. He couldn't help it. He didn't know who had made the ship or what it signi-fied, but the fact that something so whimsical, so

singular, could exist filled him with an unaccustomed sense of joy.

He thought back to what he'd told the girl,
Essie. Perhaps he should take his own advice. Perhaps it was time to stop running and return to old
friends.

The prospect filled Murtagh with a mess of
conflicting emotions. Wherever he'd gone, he
had heard the venom in people's voices when
they spoke his name. No matter how vigorously
Eragon or Nasuada might defend him in public,
few there were who would trust him after his actions in service to Galbatorix. It was a bitter, un-
fair truth—one that circumstances had long ago
forced him to accept.

Because of it, he had hidden his face, changed
his name, and kept to the fringes of settled land,
never walking where others might know him.
And while the time alone had done both him and
Thorn good, it was no way to live the rest of their

lives. So again he wondered if perhaps the time had come to turn and face his past.

But first . . . Murtagh looked down at the object he was holding: the bird-skull amulet he'd taken off Sarros's neck.

What sort of enchantment had been placed on it that could withstand the Name of Names? Magic without words was a wild, dangerous thing, and rare was the spellcaster brave or foolish enough to tamper with it. He had not even dared use it himself in the Fulsome Feast, not with so many innocent bystanders nearby.

No, before anything else, Murtagh decided he would like to find the witch-woman Bachel and ask her a few questions. The answers, he suspected, would be most interesting.

✦ ✦ ✦

CHAPTER III

The Hall of Colors

It was night when Eragon returned to himself, and the only illumination in the Hall of Colors came from the flameless lanterns on the walls and the inner radiance of the Eldunarí themselves.

He sat staring at the floor while he regrouped and recovered. A smile spread across his face. *Murtagh!* Eragon hadn't heard anything from his half brother since they'd parted outside of Urû'baen, now Ilirea, after the death of Galbatorix. Rumors of a red dragon seen flying here or there throughout Alagaësia had been the only clues that Murtagh was still alive. It was good to know he was doing well—or at least better than before.

He deserves to be happy, Eragon thought.

Then he paused to consider the subject of Murtagh's search, as well as the witch-woman Bachel. Both concerned him, for they reminded Eragon of how much he still didn't know about Alagaësia and its denizens. Ignorance wasn't a flaw he could afford anymore; it could too easily prove fatal for those he and Saphira had sworn to protect.

He hoped Murtagh would be careful. Wherever he was going, Eragon felt sure it would be dangerous in the extreme. Murtagh was plenty capable, but he wasn't invulnerable. No one was.

Again, Eragon heard Murtagh's advice to Essie: "Sometimes you have to stand and fight. Sometimes running away isn't an option." And Eragon knew then why the dragons had shown him that particular vision.

His smile returned, and he let out his breath. If a girl like Essie could stand her ground and face the difficulties of her life, so too could he—and with good grace. He was a Dragon Rider, after all. It was what he was supposed to do.

Besides, none of the problems he was wrestling with were half so unpleasant or daunting as that nasty Hjordis. Eragon chuckled and shook his head, glad he wasn't the one having to deal with the spoiled girl.

Did that help? Glaedr asked.

Eragon nodded, although the dragon couldn't see, and stood, stretching his sore legs. *Yes. It did. Thank you, Ebrithil. . . . All of you, thank you.*

A chorus of answering thoughts was his reply: *You are welcome, youngling.*

One day the dragons would no longer consider

him an unseasoned whelp, but today was not that day. A wry expression on his face, Eragon took his leave and climbed back up the ramp of stairs to the eyrie.

Outside, cold stars shone down upon Mount Arngor and the lands below. The sight reminded Eragon of the grass ship Murtagh had seen—the same ship Arya had made one night by a fire, when she'd come to help him escape on foot from the Empire. That had also been the night when a group of wilding spirits had emerged from the dark and, during a visitation, transformed a lily into a flower of living gold.

Arya had imbued the ship with a spell to draw energy from the plants beneath so that it might always stay aloft and the grass would remain fresh and green forevermore. It gladdened Eragon to know the ship was still out there, sailing around Alagaësia upon waves of wind, and he wondered

at everything it had seen in its wanderings. Just
another mystery among so many others.

Saphira was waiting for him, curled in her
nest. She opened an eye as Eragon undressed and
crawled under her near wing. *So?* she said.

"You were right," Eragon said, settling against
the warmth of her belly. "I needed a break."

A low humming formed in her chest. *You're
much nicer when you're not snapping like an angry fox.*

He chuckled. "True." Then he shared with her
the vision from the Eldunarí.

Afterward, she said, *I would like it if Murtagh
and Thorn came to stay with us.*

"So would I."

*Do you think we have another enemy hidden in
Alagaësia?*

"I don't know. If we do, they're just one more
added to the lot. I wouldn't worry about it."

No. . . . She took a deep breath and shuffled

her wings as she readjusted her position. *No more worries for tonight. Leave them for the morning.*

"No more worries," Eragon agreed with a smile. He closed his eyes and snuggled closer, and for the first time since they'd arrived at Mount Arngor, he put aside his concerns and slept without anxiety or interruption.

PART TWO

The Witch

CHAPTER IV

Rhymes and Riddles

Eragon stared across his desk at Angela the herbalist, studying her.

She was sitting in the dark pinewood chair
the elves had sung for him, still clad in her furs
and travel cloak. Flakes of melted snow beaded
the tips of the rabbit-hair trim, bright and shiny
by the light of the lanterns.

On the floor next to the herbalist lay the
werecat, Solembum, in his feline form, licking
himself dry. His tongue rasped loudly against his
shaggy coat.

Billows of snow swirled past the open windows of the eyrie, blocking the view. Some slipped in and dusted the sills, but for the most part, the wards Eragon had set kept out the snow and cold.

The storm had settled on Mount Arngor two days past, and it still showed no signs of letting up. Nor was it the first. Winter on the eastern plains had been far harsher than Eragon expected. Something to do with the effects of the Beor Mountains on the weather, he suspected.

Angela and Solembum had arrived with the latest batch of traders: a group of bedraggled humans, travel-worn and half frozen to death. Accompanying the herbalist had also been the dragon-marked child Elva—she who carried the curse of self-sacrifice Eragon had inadvertently laid upon her. A curse instead of a blessing, and every time he saw her, he still felt a sense of responsibility.

They'd left the girl on the lower levels, eating with the dwarves. She'd grown since Eragon had last seen her, and now she looked to be nearly ten, which was at least six years in advance of her actual age.

"Now then, where's the clutch of bouncing baby dragons I was expecting?" said Angela. She pulled off her mittens and then folded her hands over her knee and matched his gaze. "Or have they still not hatched?"

Eragon resisted the urge to grimace. "No. The main part of the hold is far from finished— as you've seen—and stores are tight. To quote Glaedr, the eggs have already waited for a hundred years; they can wait one more winter."

"Mmm, he might be right. Be careful of waiting too long, though, Argetlam. The future belongs to those who seize it. What about Saphira, then?"

"What about her?"

"Has she laid any eggs?"

Eragon shifted, uncomfortable. The truth was Saphira hadn't, not yet, but he didn't want to admit as much. The information felt too personal to share. "If you're so interested, you should ask her yourself."

The herbalist cocked her head. "Oh, touchy, are we? I suppose I will, then."

"What brings you here, and in the middle of winter, no less?"

She produced a small copper flask from under her cloak and took a sip before offering it to Eragon. He shook his head. "Now, now, King-slayer, you almost sound as if you're not happy to see us."

"You are always welcome at our hearth," said Eragon, choosing his words with care. The last thing he wanted to do was offend this quicksilver-like woman. "But you can't deny it's odd, venturing out across the plains in the dead months of the year. I'm just curious. You of all people should understand that."

"My, how far we've come from that day in Teirm," Angela murmured. Then she raised her voice again: "Two reasons. First, because I'm currently on a take-around with Elva. I thought it would do both her and me some good to leave the human parts of Alagaësia for a time. Especially seeing as how Nasuada's pet spellcasters in Du Vrangr Gata are making life difficult for harmless, innocent hedge witches such as myself."

"Harmless? Innocent?" Eragon raised an eyebrow.

"Well," said Angela, and her lips quirked with a smile, "perhaps not so harmless as all that. In any case, we've been to Du Weldenvarden. We've been to the dream well in Mani's Caves, and we've stopped over in Tronjheim. Fell Thindarë seemed the next natural destination. Besides . . ." She fiddled with the trim of her cloak. "It occurred to me that Elva might be able to help you soothe the minds of some of the Eldunarí."

Eragon nodded, reading the meaning between her lines. "That she might. And . . . were I to venture a guess, I would say she might learn something by it also."

"Exactly," said Angela with unexpected force. She wiped the water off the fur of her hood, not meeting his eyes. "Exactly."

A deeper concern began to form in Eragon. Of all the people and creatures he had met since discovering Saphira's egg in the Spine so long ago, Elva was perhaps the most dangerous. His badly worded blessing had forced her to become something more than human: a living shield against the misfortune of others. As a result, Elva had gained the ability to foresee and thus forestall impending hurts. Nor was that the end to her powers. She could perceive the most painful thoughts in those around her, which was an intimidating—even frightening—prospect. And for a young child to bear that burden: overwhelming.

It never ceased to amaze Eragon that, despite his spell, Elva had retained her sanity. She was still young, though, and risks remained.

"What are you not saying, Angela?" he said, narrowing his eyes and leaning forward. "Has something gone amiss with Elva?"

"Amiss?" The herbalist laughed, bright and merry. "No, nothing *amiss*. You have an overly suspicious mind, Shadeslayer."

"Hmm." He wasn't convinced.

The rasping of Solembum's tongue continued unabated.

Then the herbalist reached under her cloak and removed a thin, flat packet wrapped in oilskin. "Second: my other reason for coming." She handed Eragon the packet. "In light of my impending dotage, I decided to put pen to paper and write an account of my life. An autobiography of sorts, if you will."

"Your impending dotage, eh?" The curly-haired woman didn't look any older than her early twenties. Eragon hefted the packet. "And what am I supposed to do with this?"

"Read it, of course!" said Angela. "Why else would I traipse across the whole of Alagaësia and beyond but to get the informed opinion of a man raised as an illiterate farmer?"

Eragon eyed her for a long moment. "Very funny." He unwrapped the packet to find a small collection of rune-covered pages, each written with a different color of ink. Shuffling through them, he saw several chapter titles. The numbers appended to them varied wildly. "There are parts missing," he said.

The herbalist fluttered her hand, as if the matter was of no consequence. "That's because

I'm writing them out of order. It's how my brain works."

"But how do you know that"—he squinted at a page—"this is supposed to be chapter one hundred twenty-five and not, say, one hundred twenty-three?"

"Because," said Angela with a superior expression, "I have faith in the gods, and they reward my devotion."

"No, you don't," said Eragon. He leaned forward, feeling as if he'd just gained the advantage in a sparring match. "You don't have faith in anyone but yourself."

She made an expression of mock outrage. "Here now! You dare question my conviction, Shur'tugal?!"

"Not at all. I just question where it's directed. Even if I took your word at its face, what gods do you have faith in? Those of the dwarves? The Urgals? The wandering tribes?"

Angela's smile broadened. "Why, all of them, of course. My faith is not so narrow as to be restricted to a single set of deities."

"I imagine that would be quite . . . contradictory."

"You're far too literal-minded for your own good, Bromsson, as I've told you before. Expand your conception of what is or isn't possible." She eyed him with an aggravating amount of amusement.

"Perhaps you're right," he said, attempting to indulge her. "Still, the gods didn't write these pages."

"No, I did. But now we're getting distracted by theology, and while it makes for delightful conversation, that's not my intent. . . . Are you familiar with the puzzle rings the dwarves make?"

Eragon nodded, remembering the one Orik had given him during their trip from Tronjheim to the elven city of Ellesméra.

"Then you know how, when they're disassembled, they look like a patternless bunch of twisted bands. But arrange them in the right sequence, and hey ho! there you go—a beautiful, solid ring." Angela gestured toward the papers in his hand. "Order or disorder: it depends on your perspective."

"And what perspective is yours?" he asked softly.

"That of the ring maker," she answered in an equally soft tone.

"I—"

"Stop asking so many questions and read the manuscript." She picked up her mittens and stood. "We'll talk after."

As the herbalist left the eyrie, Solembum stopped his licking, stared at Eragon with his slitted eyes, and said, *Beware of shadows that walk, human. There are strange forces at work in the world.*

Then the werecat left as well, padding away on silent paws.

Annoyed and a little disquieted, Eragon settled back in his chair and started to read from Angela's papers. The contrary part of him was tempted to read them out of sequence, just to spite her, but he behaved himself and started as he should, from the beginning. . . .

✦ ✦ ✦

CHAPTER V

On the Nature of Stars

PREFACE

Many have deemed me a frivolous person, and that is just as I like it. When I was young (and yes, dear reader, I was once young—disregard the foolish words to the contrary from those followers of the Doctrine of the Residue), I made the error of showing myself to others. And in my youthful enthusiasm, I repeated the mistake a grave many times.

Do you wish to poke and pry, to see and know, to taste my soul? I am no capering child. No.

Now I make mistakes rarely, and do not repeat them, for the mistakes of my profession come with a price measured in blood and flesh and lives.

So.

The tales contained in this volume are all true, and every one is false. I leave it to the discerning reader to untangle the contrary strands of history, memory, facts, and lies. I will say this: care has been taken to provide an accurate telling of the most well-known—and hence, most misunderstood and ill-reported—events here recounted.

The truth rarely lies in the middle, somewhere between two opposing viewpoints. In my experience, it is far more likely to be found a good deal above and to the left of the apparent, much-proclaimed "truths." Look up from the plane of human dealings and you may see a dragon flying overhead—or at least an informative sky that warns you to take cover before the arrival of a storm.

Many will advise you to dig for the truth, but you must never, never do that. I have dug. I have seen what lies below, and I would not wish that upon the worst of you.

Strive for wisdom! Or at least a decrease in idiocy.

—*Angela of Many Names*

CHAPTER 7

The stars move across the night sky.

When I was a child, this was an obvious truth, something not even worth thinking about—like the rise of the sun or the change of the seasons.

I vividly recall that night spent lying on my back in the high hill pasture, eyes wide open to the celestial show. The burning stars brought a cold glow across the whole clear sky, so far from the smoke of the town-fires and the light of the searchers' torches.

The stars trace their nightly paths over the land. They move. It is so obvious; how could it not be true? But the obvious is often an illusion.

The seeding grass and late spring flowers were black silhouettes against the star-bright sky. The greenery was high enough to hide a heifer, thus giving the impression that I was peering up from the bottom of a hole. Even if the searchers came to this pasture, they could not have seen me from mere feet away.

As hours passed, the stars turned above, night chill drew the heat from my body, and I fell into a curious trance, not asleep—I did not dare close my eyes—but not fully awake. Thinking of it now, it is obvious what natural processes were affecting my body, but for many years, they were mysterious to me.

The world *altered*.

In a moment, I felt as if everything—the earth beneath my back, under my outstretched arms and palms pressed flat against the damp ground—became insubstantial. I was falling away from nothing and into nothing. My body had no weight and was both plummeting and floating and yet was still pressed into the ground. My perception of time changed. The stars seemed to speed across the sky, until I suddenly felt as if they were static and I was moving. The ground, the trees and mountains, everything was moving.

I had no concept of "planet" then, but that was the right word, had I known it.

Dawn brightened the sky, and still, I had no perception of time passing. Then, with the first rays of sunlight, the trance broke and I returned to myself with a shaken understanding of the world, and a new resolution to face the inevitable troubles . . . *consequences* that were soon to strike.

CHAPTER 23

The stars are stationary;
the rotation of the planet
creates the illusion of stellar motion.

With the barest touch of a single finger, the globe silently spun on nearly frictionless dwarven bearings. It was a beautiful, glittering thing of near-microscopic details incised into some unknown pale metal. Even the grandest geographical features of the world were reduced to tiny bumps and dips of cold metal under my fingertips. Doubtless, my careless touch grazed over many a place I have since visited.

I had felt a powerful fascination with the globe from the time I first set eyes on it. I had longed to study it for hours and days, to compare its features with familiar maps and learn about the different methods of representing a round object on a flat surface.

Though the globe was—I now know—a hopelessly incomplete depiction of our planet, it nevertheless was a captivating work of art, and I regret its destruction. A small price to pay . . . but still, art should be protected.

But in that moment, the globe was a mere distraction that stole precious seconds.

Time was limited. The library could Shift at any moment, and the longer I lingered, the greater the probability that I would be stranded in some unknowable hinterland, some other space, neither here nor there.

The inner door of the library only coincided with the outer door at particular moments, and I did not yet have the skill to perform the obscure computations required to predict the times of safe passage. It was an ingenious system for protecting the most precious of secrets. Regardless of the dangers, I was determined to take those first steps down the path to true knowledge.

Overstaying the window of time that the library and the tower were connected was not my greatest fear, though. I was preoccupied by the possibility of being discovered in the library by *him*.

The Keeper of the Tower had bought my apprenticeship with the promise of education, but the initial trickle of information had slowed to an occasional drip, just enough to wet my lips, and I needed to drink deep, to plunge and swim and drown.

My disgust at that betrayal and desire for justice outweighed my dread of the consequences of being caught, but just barely. I needed to know, and stolen freedom is still freedom.

Without the Keeper present, doling out simple books full of concepts I had long since mastered, the library felt far larger than I remembered. The carvings on the towering shelves seemed to move ever so slightly at the edges of my vision, though never when directly observed.

I searched swiftly, without further distraction, but with increasing desperation and lack of attention to my carefully prepared plan. I tipped back book after book: plain and gilded, narrower than a finger and wider than a hand, some improbably heavy for their sizes.

click

It was an unremarkable tome that triggered the hidden drawer in a nearby bookcase—along with the thrill that accompanies something unpredictable but much anticipated. I lunged toward the drawer and, in my haste, toppled a flameless lantern from its stand.

It did not break.

It did not activate an alarm.

But it did cost precious seconds as I struggled

to right it with excitement-clumsy fingers. My terror of leaving any evidence of my intrusion was poorly weighed against the danger of being trapped.

Would there have been enough time without that error? Without the momentary contemplation of the globe? Or perhaps the venture was doomed from the start by my inexperience.

All the gold in the world is worthless if you are wandering in an endless desert without a supply of water. What value do the secrets of the universe have if you are lost somewhere beyond the influence of known powers?

The library *Shifted*. And it felt like nothing and everything. The library looked exactly as before, but my entire body ached in resonance with the sudden wrongness in the underlying fabric of the universe. I was in the same place and yet vastly elsewhere.

I was trapped.

CHAPTER 125

All matter in the universe is in motion;
all motion is relative.

"It is time."

"It is always *a* time."

I nodded. Elva invariably saw things in such a pleasantly askew way. After the heartbreak with Bilna, the idea of trying to teach another had long repulsed me. But more and more, I had been thinking of Elva's potential to be my apprentice, and obversely, of what she could become without guidance.

The walls, ceiling, and floor of her chambers in the citadel of Ilirea were lavishly draped with fabrics, giving the impression of being within a tent, or perhaps the belly of some textile beast. She sat in a nest of pillows, comfortably threatening. She had grown sharper and longer since my last visit.

"You know why I have come," I said.

"Of course. You have heard of the latest . . . *intrigues*." She imbued the word with poison.

I sat opposite her, on the overlapping carpets that covered the entire floor of the chamber. "I heard that Nasuada no longer allows you to go into the city. Perhaps you are banned from parts of the citadel. Perhaps your world is restricted to just these rooms."

The girl eyed me with something akin to contempt. "No one can keep me imprisoned. You know that. I stay in my quarters because I prefer it. I can leave whenever I want."

"Theoretically, but then you would have the annoyance of constant pursuit. It wouldn't take much for a member of Du Vrangr Gata to catch you unawares—while you are sleeping, for example—and bring you back."

"Bah. You don't understand. Begone and good

riddance to you." She waved a hand at me and turned away.

"I have heard stories—no doubt expanded in the telling—of your little outbursts, your . . . demonstrations. I cannot blame Nasuada for trying to contain you. Trade negotiations set back by weeks, fights breaking out, the most important food supplier to the army found dishonoring the dwarven chapel—"

"He was waiting for a friend."

"He had forgotten his clothes."

"It could happen to anyone."

"Making the elven ambassador cry? In front of the Urgals?"

Elva laughed. "That was fun."

"You show them too much, and they will use it against you. I come here with an offer of help, if you want it."

Elva just stared, a wise conversational technique that I recommend in a great many situations.

I continued: "If I could take you from this place without anyone knowing, would you come?"

Her chin lifted. "Why? So you can spy on me for Eragon? So you can treat me like a dangerous animal that needs to be kept on a chain? So you can use me for some petty little plans? I've learned so much, so quickly. People are fragile—poke them here or there and watch them crumble. I don't need your help."

"Oh, you wish to be persuaded, is that it?"

Again, an unblinking stare was her only response.

"Very well. Eragon removing the compulsion to help did not improve your life as you wished. You are stretching your wings, testing your abilities, and trying to find a place in the world. But with each expansion and experiment, you are reminded again that you will never fit in and just be seen as you." Not a question, a statement. A needle to prick and provoke. An effective one: Elva's

face hardened, revealing only the tiniest spark of
the raging flames behind her eyes.

"Everyone wants things they can't have, don't
they? Even you?"

"Oh yes." I couldn't help but smile, though it
doubtless incensed her further. "Elva . . . you know
the game, but just the opening moves. I can show
you so many things and keep you safe until such
time as you choose to return to this life. The span
and depth of existence is far greater than anyone
can know—not even the oldest dragon or the
wisest elf. I have seen more than most, but even
that is less than a particle of dust, smaller than the
smallest thing, and then smaller still."

Elva bit her lip, for once looking like a normal
child.

Ah, there it was. The vastness of everything
would not persuade her. But it did achieve the
first step: reinforce her perception of my mastery.
So, time for her real desire.

"I have made myself immune to your abil-ity, so I can offer you a time of peace from all the suffering that constantly impinges on your mind. You can learn who you are and what you want to be. And when you return, you will have a new command over your life. Yes, there will be boundaries and restrictions while you are by my side. But I don't need the power derived from your curse, Elva. I have no need to break or bend you."

She gave me a look, such a look—hope when hope is not allowed, hope poisoned by profound bitterness. "Easy words," she said.

"Am I lying?"

"You know I can't see when people are lying!"

"Yes. You must choose with incomplete infor-mation, just like everyone else. Do you wish to come with me, Elva? Think carefully. I will not return again with this offer." Then it was my turn to stare and wait for a response.

In any other child, Elva's deep scowl would presage a tantrum, but her control did not weaken. "Do you really think the guards would let you take me? Ha! In just the last fortnight, they've stopped two attempts to steal me away." Anger made her usually cool, contemptuous tone waver.

I made no attempt to hide my unease. "I hadn't heard. Then your departure is all the more important; I suspect that dangerous groups are determined to have you as a weapon."

"Ha!"

"I know. They have no understanding of your power, though they believe they do. And what people think they understand, they think they can control."

"I'm not going to hide who and what I am."

"There is great value in stealth; you have already attracted much attention."

"Oh! I have guessed your plan. You will have me talk my way past the guards. But it won't work;

they are warded against me. They're afraid of me."

And there was a deeply worrying touch of pride in Elva's voice.

"Neither the guards stationed outside nor the heavy wards on the room mean a thing if I want to take you from within these walls," I said.

Elva made a scornful noise.

"Just tell me, do you wish to go?"

"What I wish has never mattered, not from the moment that Eragon spoke his words."

"Do you wish to go?"

"What is your plan? Invisibility? Addling the guards' brains? Tunneling through the floor? None of those things will work."

"No. I will simply open a door and we will walk away. Nothing more."

"*Ha!*" Proper disgust this time.

I stood. "For the last time, do you wish to go?"

"Yes! A thousand curses on you, for making me want things. Yes."

"Then come." I held out my hand, but Elva did not accept it.

Without assistance, she climbed out of her nest of pillows. "Fine. But I still think you are lying. They've planned for every possible way out of here."

But not, I thought, *the impossible ways.*

There was so much work to do with Elva, yet I found myself oddly looking forward to it. She had great potential to understand the incomprehensible. "Gather what you wish to bring, and we will go."

Though she was clearly skeptical in the extreme, Elva put a small wooden cask and a miscellany of oddments on a blanket and tied it into a bundle.

"What of your caretaker, Greta?" I asked.

"I've seen to it she will live in comfort the rest of her years."

"That is good of you, but events are often

unpredictable. You might never get the chance to see her again. Forestall future regrets by saying a proper farewell now."

Elva hesitated, but in the end, she did as I recommended. Not wanting to be seen, lest someone later rummage through Greta's memories, I slipped behind a fold of drapery while the girl rang a bell.

Greta arrived quickly, ever attentive to the needs of her charge. She was understandably distressed by Elva's farewells; the old woman was utterly devoted to the girl and had sacrificed much to protect her. I admired the tenacity and determination with which Greta had pursued her purpose. When she spoke of her fears—that Elva was far too young to go unprotected into the world—Elva assured her that she would be safe and thanked her for all she had done.

But Greta would not be dismissed. She talked in circles, returning to the same points again and again—how she loved, was proud of, and wanted to protect Elva—as she struggled to express the depth of her feelings.

Elva's responses grew snappish as her care-taker continued. Then she became quiet, and I was concerned. I was about to intercede when Elva said something softly, and Greta shrieked a horrible strangled sound, like some dying animal.

Whatever fear Elva had given voice to, it struck her caretaker a near mortal blow. But then the girl murmured again, and Greta exclaimed again, but in a very different tone.

"You monstrous . . . *thing!* You can't break something and mend it a moment later with pretty words. Broken things stay broken. Wounds heal into scars, not skin. I love you. I love you so much. Do you even know what that means? I will love you and worry for you with every breath in my body, so long as I live, but I will never again trust you."

After brief shuffling sounds, the door moaned closed, and then the room was terribly quiet.

I stepped out from my hiding place. "Was that really necessary?"

Elva shrugged, trying to appear unaffected by the consequences of her actions, but she was pale and shaking. Then she looked me in the eye and, in just a few words, spoke my deepest fear.

Although I live every moment with the knowledge, hearing someone else say it—even without understanding the implication or meaning—felt like being stung by a thousand wasps, countless stabs of fear and surprise and pain.

I should have been safe from her power, but somehow the curse had circumvented my wards. Again and again, the deep magic of the dragons tried to fulfill its purpose, finding ways around even the strongest protections. I resolved to redouble my wards as soon as possible, to forestall Elva's prying powers, at least for a time.

She looked up at me, defiant, and said, "Do you really want to travel with me, witch? Can you bear to be around me, knowing that I know?"

But she could not break my composure. I was not the inquisitive child I once had been, not the foolish apprentice or the sharp-edged postulant. During both the broken days of wandering and the times of pleasant stasis, this fear had controlled me. Those days were past; now I could confront it without flinching. I had pondered for years and learned to admit, if not accept, the truth of the straightness of right angles.

A strange series of emotions passed over Elva's face, as my reaction was not what she had expected. Unlike Greta, I had long since mastered my feelings.

I said, "You cannot turn me from my purpose. I have braved far more dangerous things than you. As you should know . . . Now, time is pressing. Come."

Elva hugged the bundle of possessions to her chest. "Can you really take us from here?" And she fixed me with a powerful glare that implied: *Now disappoint me, adult. . . . All the others have; why wouldn't you?*

I once more extended my hand. This time Elva took it. I led her to a wall and pushed aside the layers of fabric to expose the bare stone.

"What—"

I traced a line on the wall, reached out, and opened a door that wasn't there. On the other side—nighttime, a beach by a black ocean lit only by stars, so many, *many* stars, more stars than there should be.

Of course, I would not take Elva to my home, not yet. But this was a waypoint, a place to build and learn and grow. A place where she could rest her weary mind, free from the painful distraction of other people's needs.

She stared into the gap, the impossible portal. No cutting words this time.

Solembum sauntered into view and peered around the edge of the doorway, into Elva's chamber. He twitched his tasseled ears and looked up at me.

I'm hungry. Did you bring food?

Of course. Rabbit this time. Does that meet with your approval?

A sniff. *It'll do.* He meandered down the beach, out of view.

"Do you wish to go?" I asked a final time.

Elva squeezed my hand as tightly as she could. She walked through the door, and I followed a half step behind.

✦ ✦ ✦

CHAPTER VI

Questions and Answers

Eragon lowered the sheaf of pages and stared for a long while into the whirling snow outside the eyrie.

Still holding the papers, he stood and descended the long curve of stairs that led to the common area at the base of the stone finger. The dwarves were there eating, and most of the humans as well, but only a few of the elves and none of the Urgals. In a corner, one of the dwarves was playing a bone flute carved with runes, and the deep, thoughtful melody provided a homely accompaniment to the murmur of conversation.

The herbalist was sitting by herself next to one of the fires, knitting the brim for a woolen cap made of red and green yarn. She looked up as Eragon approached, but the speed of her clicking needles never slowed or faltered.

"I have questions," he said.

"Then you have more wisdom than most."

He squatted next to her and tapped the pages. "How much of this is true?"

Angela laughed a little, and her breath frosted in the cold. "I believe I made that perfectly clear in my preface. It's as true or not true as you want it to be."

"So you made it all up."

"No," she said, giving him a serious look over her flashing needles. "I did not. Even if I had, there are often lessons worth learning in stories. Wouldn't you agree?"

Eragon shook his head, bemused and somewhat exasperated. He pulled over a stump they were using for a chair, sat, and stretched his legs out toward the fire. He thought about how Brom would often smoke his pipe in the evenings, and for a moment, Eragon considered getting a pipe of his own. The dwarves would be sure to have one he could use. . . .

In a quiet voice, he said, "Why did you have me read this?"

"Perhaps because I think there are certain doors you need to walk through."

He frowned, frustrated as always with the herbalist's answers. "The Keeper of the Tower, is he—"

"I have nothing to say about him." Eragon opened his mouth again, and Angela interrupted: "No. Ask other questions if you must, but not about *him.*"

"As you wish." But Eragon's suspicions remained. He looked across the common area. Elva was there, sitting and chatting with a group of dwarves, all of whom were attending to her with uncharacteristic animation. "What you wrote about her . . ."

"Elva is a bright young woman with a bright future," said Angela, and she gave him an overly bright smile.

"In that case, I should see to it that she has the sort of training that a young person of such great promise *ought* to have."

"Exactly," said Angela, seeming both satisfied and relieved. Then she surprised him by saying, "Understand me, Eragon; it's not that the task is beyond me, but some tasks are best accomplished with more than one set of hands."

He nodded. "Of course. Elva is my responsibility, after all."

"That she is. . . . Although you could blame her on Brom, if you wanted, for not teaching you the proper forms of the ancient language."

Eragon chuckled, despite himself. "Perhaps,

but blaming the dead for our mistakes never accomplishes much."

The clacking of the herbalist's needles continued at the same steady pace as she gave him a thoughtful look and said, "My, you have grown wise in your old age."

"Not really. I'm just trying to avoid making the same mistakes as before."

"One could argue that is the definition of wisdom."

He half smiled. "One could, but just avoiding mistakes isn't enough to make a person wise. Does a turtle that lives alone under a rock for a hundred years really learn anything?"

Angela shrugged. "Does a man who lives alone in a tower for a hundred years learn anything?"

Eragon eyed her for a moment. "Maybe. It depends."

"Even so."

He stood and held out the papers toward her. "Here."

"Keep them. They will serve you better than me. And besides, I have the words in my head already. That's all that really matters."

"I'll make sure they're stored where no one will ever think to look," he said. He tucked the pages into the front of his jerkin.

She smiled. "You do that."

Then Eragon looked back at Elva, and a hint of trepidation stirred within him. He ignored it. Just because something was difficult or uncomfortable didn't mean it wasn't worth doing. "We'll talk later," he said, and Angela made a noncommittal sound.

As Eragon walked across the common area, he reached out with his mind to Saphira, who was outside with Blödhgarm and a number of the elves, clearing snow with the fire from her throat.

You've been listening? he said.

Of course, little one.

I could use your help, I think.

On my way.

And he felt her turn and head inward. Pleased, Eragon continued on. The witch-child might prove troublesome for him alone, but even she would hesitate to disregard a dragon. Moreover, Eragon did not believe that the girl would be able to manipulate Saphira with her powers the way she might him.

Either way, it would be an interesting experience.

As he stopped in front of Elva, she looked up at him with her violet eyes and smiled, wide and sharp-toothed, like a cat before a mouse. "Greetings, Eragon," she said.

PART THREE

The Worm

CHAPTER VII

Deadfall

At long last, spring had come to Mount Arngor.

Eragon was outside the main hall, grubbing up roots from several plots of dirt along the edge of the surrounding forest. Once cleared, the plots would be planted with herbs, vegetables, berries, and other useful crops, including cardus weed for the dwarves and humans to smoke and fireweed to help dragons better digest their food.

He'd taken his shirt off and was enjoying the noonday sun on his skin. It was a welcome plea-sure amid weather that was still often cold and cloudy. Saphira lounged nearby, basking on a bed of trampled grass. Before he started, she'd raked the plots with her claws to break up the soil, which made the work far easier.

With Eragon were several dwarves: two male, three female, all from Orik's clan, the Dûrgrimst Ingeitum. As they worked, they laughed and sang in their language, and Eragon sang along with them as best he could. He had been trying to learn something of Dwarvish in his limited spare time. Also the Urgals' even harsher tongue. As the ancient language had taught him, words were power. Sometimes literally, sometimes figuratively, but either way, Eragon wanted to know and understand everything he could, both for his own benefit and the benefit of those he was now responsible for.

A memory came to him then: *He was standing in a small meadow near the outskirts of Ellesméra, surrounded by the pine trees sung into graceful shapes*

*by the elves. A treasure trove of flowers lay before
him, growing in flowing patterns within that grassy
oasis amid the shadowed forest. Bees hummed among
the profusion of blossoms, and butterflies flitted about
the clearing, like petals given flight. Beneath him, his
shadow was that of a dragon, flecked with the refracted
light from his ruddy scales.*

And all was right. And all was good.

Eragon shook himself as he returned to the
present. Drops of sweat flew from his face. Ever
since the Eldunarí had opened their minds and
shared their memories with him, he had been
experiencing flashes of recollection not his own.
The bursts were disorienting, both on account of
their unexpectedness and because he had grasped
only a small part of the great storehouse of knowledge now packed into his head. To fully master it
would be the task of a lifetime.

That was okay. Learning was one of Eragon's
chief pleasures, and he still had so much to learn

about history, Alagaësia, the dragons, and life in general.

That particular memory had come from a dragon named Ivarros, who—as Eragon thought back—had lost his body in an unseasonably strong thunderstorm before the fall of the Riders.

The images from outside Ellesméra caused Eragon to pause and remember his own time in the elven city. A slight twinge of heartsickness formed in his chest as he thought of Arya, now queen of her people in the ancient forest of Du Weldenvarden. They had spoken several times through the scrying mirrors he kept in the hold's eyrie, but both he and she were busy with their duties, and their conversations had been few and far between.

Saphira eyed him from underneath hooded lids. Then she snorted, sending a small puff of smoke rolling across the ground.

Eragon smiled and hoisted his pick overhead

again. Life was good. Winter had broken. The main hall was finished, with the roof now sealed. More chambers were nearing completion. Three of the formerly mad Eldunarí had been moved from the caves below into the Hall of Colors, as a direct result of Elva applying her particular talents.

The girl and the herbalist and the werecat had departed two weeks previously. While Eragon was not sorry to see them go—their presence was always somewhat disquieting—he was proud of the time he'd spent with Elva. He had worked with the girl every day since her arrival, training her as Brom and Oromis had trained him. She had also spent long hours with Saphira, Glaedr, and several of the other—sane—dragons. By the time she and Angela departed, Eragon could already see a change in her attitude. Elva had appeared calmer and more relaxed, and some of the sting had dissipated from her responses.

Eragon just hoped the improvements would stick.

When he'd asked where they intended to go, Angela said, "Oh, to some distant shore, I should think. A place nice and isolated, where we don't have to worry about unwelcome surprises."

Over the past few months, Eragon had done his best to ferret out more answers from the herbalist—on a range of subjects—but he might as well have tried to cut through a wall of granite with a twig. She deflected and dissembled and otherwise stymied his efforts with perfect success. The one new thing he *had* learned was the story of how she and Solembum had first met—and that had made for a most entertaining evening indeed.

A strip of pink amid the overturned soil caught Eragon's attention. He lowered his pick and crouched down to see a long, banded earthworm feeling its way across the clumps of fragrant earth.

"Here now," he said, feeling sorry for having

disturbed the worm's home. He put his hand in front of the worm and allowed it to crawl onto his palm. Then he lifted the worm out of the plot, carried it a few feet away, and set it down near a clump of dry grass, where it might burrow back into the ground.

Shouts rang out from within the main hall: "Ebrithil! Ebrithil!" The elf Ästrith emerged from the shadowed doorway, covered in dirt and dust, a bloody scrape along her right forearm and a strained expression on her face.

The nape of Eragon's neck prickled, old instincts taking hold. He sprinted back to the plot, grabbed the pick, and ran to Ästrith even as she said, "The tunnel we were working in collapsed. Two of—"

"Which tunnel?" Eragon asked, hurrying into the hall with her. Behind them, Saphira heaved herself to her feet and lumbered after.

"On the lowest level. The dwarves were trying

to reopen a branch tunnel they found yesterday. The ceiling gave way, and two of them are trapped beneath the stones."

"Did you tell Blödhgarm?"

"He will meet us there."

Eragon grunted.

Together, they crossed the main hall and hurried down the stairs and through the door that granted access to the mining tunnels beneath the hold. As the cold underground air hit his skin, Eragon regretted not pausing to grab his shirt. *Oh well.*

For a few silent minutes, they hurried through the switchback tunnels, descending ever deeper into the side of Mount Arngor. Lanterns had been hung on the walls at regular, but sparse, intervals, and the shadows pooled thick and heavy between them.

In the back of his mind, Eragon felt Saphira keeping close watch. She said, *How can I help?* He could sense her frustration; the tunnels were too small for a grown dragon like her.

Just stand ready. I may need your strength.

As he and Ästrith neared the lower depths of the old mine, angry voices sounded ahead of them, echoing off the bare stone in a confusing chorus. A cloud of dust still clogged the air near the collapsed section, and three separate werelights hung near the ceiling, providing additional—if unsteady—illumination.

Four dwarves emerged from the haze; Eragon recognized them all. They had been digging through the rubble, stacking the broken pieces of rock on either side of the tunnel as they attempted to excavate their buried brethren.

Ästrith pointed at a huge slab of stone that lay across the narrow passageway. Several cracks, straight as an arrow, had split the slab into sections. She said, "I broke the rock, Ebrithil, so as to lift the pieces away, but if even one part is removed, the rest will settle farther, and I am not strong enough to hold all of them at once."

The lead dwarf—a thick-bearded fellow by the name of Drûmgar—nodded. "She is right, Jurgencarmeitder. We need your help, and the help of the dragons."

Eragon placed his pick against the wall and closed his eyes for a moment. Reaching out with his mind, he searched for the buried dwarves. . . . *There.* Several feet ahead of him, a single consciousness, faint and faltering, like a candle in the wind.

Hadn't there been two dwarves trapped in the cave-in?

Eragon didn't dare wait any longer. He could feel the life ebbing from the one dwarf. "Stand clear," he said.

Ästrith and the dwarves hurried back. Then Eragon drew upon his connection with Saphira—and through her, upon the Eldunarí in the Hall of Colors—and he spoke a single word of power: "Rïsa."

The word was simple, but his intent was not, and it was intent that guided the execution of a spell.

Creaks and groans and shivering screeches rang out through the tunnel as the pile of fallen stone lifted off the ground. The cost in energy was immediate and immense; if not for the strength of the dragons, Eragon would have passed out and lost control of the spell.

Billows of fresh dust choked the air as Eragon pressed the stones back into the broken ceiling. He coughed, despite himself, and then said, "Melthna."

At his magic-borne command, all the stones he held suspended flowed together, rejoining the surrounding walls, welding themselves back to the bones of Mount Arngor. A pulse of heat— hot enough to make Eragon's cheeks sting and to singe the hairs on his chest—emanated from the now-solid casing of rocks.

He let out the breath he'd been holding and ended the spell. *Thank you,* he said to Saphira and, by extension, the Eldunarí.

As the dust settled, the wavering illumination of the werelights revealed the crumpled forms of the two dwarves lying in the tunnel ahead. Smears of blood surrounded them.

Drûmgar and the rest of the dwarves rushed toward their fallen compatriots. Eragon followed more slowly, still feeling the effects of the weirding he had wrought.

Then the dwarves groaned and began to pull at their beards and hair as they filled the mine with their lamentations. Eragon's heart sank at the sound. Again he reached out with his mind, searching for any sign of life in the two broken bodies.

Nothing. Both were dead.

Fast as he'd been, he had still failed to save

them. Eragon dropped to his knees, blinking back
a sudden upwelling of tears. The names of the two
dwarves were Nál and Brimling, and although
Eragon hadn't known them well, he'd seen them
about the fire on many a late evening, and they
had always been quick with a song or a joke and
generally full of good cheer.

Ästrith put a hand on his shoulder, but it was
a small comfort.

Eragon bent his head and let the tears fall free.
For all the spells he had learned and powers he
had gained since becoming a Dragon Rider—and
for all the strength of the dragons—some things
were still beyond him.

He could lift staggering amounts of stone with
a word, but he couldn't turn aside death. No one
could.

The rest of the day passed in a grey blur. The
dwarves took their dead to straighten their limbs,

wash their bodies, dress them in fine garments, oil their beards, and otherwise prepare them for interment in tombs of stone, as was the custom of their people.

Eragon helped Blödhgarm—who had arrived late to the tunnels—and Ästrith further secure that branch of the mine, so as to prevent any future collapses. Then, heartsore and tired, he retreated to the eyrie and cast himself down next to Saphira for a restless hour of sleep.

He still felt grim, glum, and out of joint when evening arrived. The elves attempted to console him with various high-minded phrases, but their dispassionate reasoning did little to improve his outlook. Nor were the few other humans— including Nasuada's personal envoy, one Marleth Oddsford—in any better mood. Most of them had labored hard alongside the dwarves throughout the winter, and the loss of Nál and Brimling had affected them even more than Eragon.

Yet Eragon did not forget his station. He did his duty and walked among the saddened dwarves, murmuring words of encouragement and comfort. Both Hruthmund and Drûmgar thanked him, and he promised he would attend the funerals the next day.

As the night wore on, Eragon found himself drawn to the hearth where the Urgals were gathered. They were loud and boisterous, and though they had no love for the dwarves, their leader, Skarghaz, raised his cup in honor of Nál and Brimling, and as a group, the Urgals let loose with a roar that rivaled Saphira's.

Later still, when the others had retired, Eragon remained with the Urgals, drinking *rekk*—which the Urgals made from fermented cattails—while Saphira slumbered in the corner.

"Rider!" boomed Skarghaz. "You are too sad." He was a broad, slump-shouldered Kull with long hair that he wore in a braid down his bare back.

Even in the depths of winter, he rarely deigned to put on more than a crude vest.

Eragon wasn't inclined to argue. "You are not wrong," he said, overpronouncing his words.

The massive Kull took a swig of *rekk* from his equally massive cup. Then he beckoned toward another of the Urgals: a stout, somewhat pot-bellied Urgal with a long red scar that slashed sideways across his face. "Irsk! Tell our Rider a story to settle his liver. Tell him a story of the old times."

"In *this* tongue?" Irsk replied. He grimaced, baring his fangs.

"Yes, in this tongue, *drajl*!" roared Skarghaz. And he tossed an empty cask of *rekk* at the smaller Urgal.

The cask bounced off Irsk's horns. He didn't duck or flinch, only grunted and lowered himself onto the stone floor in front of the fire. "Give me a drum, then."

At Skarghaz's order, one of the Urgals ran off to their quarters and soon returned carrying a small hide drum. Irsk set it between his legs and then paused for a moment with his thick-fingered hands resting atop the hide. He said, "I must change the words of the Urgralgra to those of your kind, Rider. They will not sound as they should, though I have studied how you speak for nigh on three winters now."

"I'm sure you will do just fine," said Eragon. He had already noticed that Irsk was more well-spoken than his fellow Urgals, and Eragon wondered if it was because Irsk had training as a bard or poet. He straightened in his chair and leaned forward, curious to hear what would come forth from the Urgal.

In the corner, Saphira cracked open her near eye to reveal a slit of gleaming blue.

Skarghaz pounded the base of his cup against his leg, splashing *rekk* across the floor. "Enough slowness, Irsk! Tell the story. Tell the one of great Kulkaras."

Again, Irsk grunted. He lowered his chin for a moment and then struck the drum a single echoing blow and began to speak.

Despite the roughness of the Urgal's words, there was a truth to them Eragon recognized. And as he listened, he felt transported to another time and place, and the events of Irsk's tale soon seemed as real as the hall itself.

✦ ✦ ✦

CHAPTER VIII

The Worm of Kulkaras

The day the dragon arrived was a day of death.

He came from the north, a shadow upon the wind. Soft and silent, he swept across the valley, blotting out the sun with his velvet wings. Where he landed, field and forest went up in flame, drifts of ash choked the streams, beasts fled—and Horned also—and the sounds of grief and terror rent the summer air.

The dragon was named Vêrmund the Grim, and he was an old and cruel dragon, canny in the ways of the world. Word of him had come from the north, but never had there been a hint or warning that he had forsaken his lair in those frozen, far-off reaches.

And yet there he was. Black as charred bone, with a polished gleam to his fitted scales and a throat packed full of fire.

The youngling, Ilgra, watched with her friends from beside the spring-fed pool where they so often swam, high in the foothills along the eastern side of the valley. From that vantage, she saw the dragon ravage their farms with fire and claw and the sweep of his jagged tail. When the warriors of Clan Skgaro attacked—attacked with bow and spear and ax— Vêrmund's flame consumed them or else he trod upon them and thus made an end to their ambitions. Even the sharpest blade could not pierce his hide, and the Skgaro had no spellcasters to aid them in battle. As such, they found themselves at the mercy of the dragon, able only to annoy or inconvenience him, but not to stop him. Never that.

Like the evil worm he was, Vêrmund ate every person who came within his reach: male and female, elder and youngling alike. None were spared. Their livestock too he ate, corralled them with fences of fire and feasted upon the helpless animals until his chops were clotted with gore and the ground a crimson shambles.

All that and more Ilgra saw. She could do nothing to help, so she stayed by the pool, though to wait hurt as much as any wound. Those of her friends who weren't so wise ran to join the fray, and of their number, many were lost.

As the dragon approached the hall of her family, Ilgra bared her teeth in a helpless snarl. Closer it came, and then closer still, and then with a slow-moving swipe, the scaled monster crushed her home.

A howl tore from Ilgra's throat, and she sank to her knees and grasped the tips of her horns.

Relief tempered her anguish as she saw her

mother scramble free of the wreckage and, with her, Ilgra's younger sister, Yhana. But it was a fleeting relief, for Vêrmund's head descended toward them, his heated maw parted.

From across the fields came sprinting Ilgra's father, spear held high. The lightness of hope filled her heart. Her father was first among the Anointed. Few there were who could match his might, and though he was small compared with the dragon, she knew his courage was equal to that of the gods'. Four winters ago, a hungry cave bear had come prowling down from the mountains, and her father had faced it with nothing more than a knife in one hand and a cudgel in the other. And he had slain the bear, killing it with a slash to the flank and a hard blow to the head.

The skull of the beast had hung over their hearth ever since.

Of everyone in Clan Skgaro, Ilgra felt sure *he* could stop Vêrmund the Grim.

Even through the tumult, Ilgra heard her father shout challenges at the dreadful dragon and curses too. With slithering quickness, Vêrmund turned to face him. Undaunted, her father darted past the worm's plow-shaped chin and drove his spear at a gap between the scales on Vêrmund's plated neck.

The blade missed, and a sound as of metal striking stone reached Ilgra from the valley floor.

Chills of mortal fear crawled along her limbs as Vêrmund uttered a thunderous chuckle, strong enough to shake the earth. The dragon's amusement angered her, and she gnashed her teeth, outraged. How dare it laugh at their misery!

To the last a warrior, her father loosed a cry and ran between Vêrmund's legs, where it was difficult for the dragon to reach.

But the creature reared back and filled the mighty bellows of his lungs, and Ilgra howled again as a torrent of blue-fringed fire engulfed her father.

Then the heaviness of despair crushed Ilgra's heart, and tears welled from her eyes.

Her father's sacrifice was not in vain, though. While he had distracted Vêrmund, her mother and sister fled the dragon, and by the blessing of Rahna the Huntress, Vêrmund showed no interest in following but concentrated instead upon their herds.

With all the clan dead or scattered, Vêrmund was free to feast at his leisure. Ilgra remained sitting on the ground, and she wept as she watched. Survivors joined her in ragged groups, their clothes scorched and torn, and some bearing fearsome wounds. Together, they huddled behind rock and ridge, silent as rabbits before a seeking snake.

Fires spread across the valley. Ranks of trees—gnarled old pines hundreds of feet tall—exploded in pillars of orange and yellow. The sound echoed among the peaks. Tails of twisting embers streamed skyward as the inferno climbed the flanks of the mountains. Billows of smoke fouled the air, and ash fell thick as snow until a false twilight blanketed the valley, a dark shroud of destruction heavy with grief, bitter with anger.

Vêrmund gorged himself upon their sheep and goats and pigs until his belly hung round and firm, pregnant with his gluttony. When finally he was sated, the dragon hove himself into the dismal sky.

He flew no great distance, though; whether because of his belly or because livestock yet remained to eat, Ilgra knew not. But the murderous old worm traveled no farther than the head of the valley. There he alighted upon the tallest mountain: high, snow-clad Kulkaras. He wrapped himself about its jagged peak, tucked his snout under his tail, and with a final, fiery sigh, closed his eyes. Thus he slept, and while he slept, he stirred no more.

Ilgra stared through the smoke toward his dark and distant bulk: a pestilential tumor mounted atop Kulkaras. As the cold constriction of hate tightened round her heart, Ilgra swore the most terrible oath she knew, for she had but one purpose now—

To kill Vêrmund the Grim. To kill the worm of Kulkaras.

▽ ▽ ▽

When last they deemed it safe, those who remained of Clan Skgaro gathered in the south of the valley, at the hall of Zhar, who tended the fish traps. Ilgra sat in a shadowed corner of the hall, chewing on her silence while the circle of old dams, the Herndall, debated what best to do. First they chose a warchief from among the males who yet lived: Arvog, the biggest, strongest, and fastest of them all. He was Anointed, as had been Ilgra's father, and he towered over those who were not. But Anointed or no, Arvog bided upon the wisdom of the dams, and it was they who decided their course.

The clan stayed huddled in Zhar's hall for a full three days, until they began to think that perhaps Vêrmund would not return. With the cruel tax of his hunger paid, and more besides, perhaps the worm had lost interest in those who had escaped. Perhaps.

While they waited, they sang the death songs for their fallen clanmates and made offerings at the shrine of Zhar to each of the gods. But most especially to Svarvok, king of the gods. For now more than ever, they needed his strength. Ilgra sang alongside her mother and sister—sang until she was a husk emptied of all but her voice—and together, they mourned their loss.

At close of the third day, the braver clan members returned to the village under cover of darkness to gather supplies and search for any wounded. They found but one: Darvek the carver, who had lost two of his fingers but otherwise still had use of his hands.

Four more days the clan held fast. In that time, Vêrmund showed no sign of movement; if not for the occasional puff of smoke that drifted from his nostrils, he might as well have been dead. Nevertheless, the clan prepared to again face the dragon. Under Arvog's direction, they made spears from saplings and arrows from dogwood, boiled leather for armor, and honed their blades. Ilgra took to the warlike preparations with enthusiasm, determined to do all she could to help defeat the dragon.

For the Herndall had decided: they would stay, the valley was theirs, and Vêrmund an intruder deserving of death. All their belongings lay in that narrow mountain cleft, under the shadow of Kulkaras. Moreover, were they to leave, they would soon trespass on the territory of rival clans, and with their numbers so diminished, the Skgaro had little hope of winning new territory by force of arms.

Vêrmund too they could not hope to defeat in open battle, but much was said around the hall fire about tricks and traps, and a sense of reckless optimism spread. The most likely way to kill the dragon, they agreed, would be to climb Kulkaras and stab him through the eye while he lay dreaming.

First, though, the dead needed reclaiming. Without the proper rites, their spirits would not find the rest they deserved, and none of the Skgaro were willing to risk being cursed by those Vêrmund had slain. Nor was fear their only spur, but sorrow and respect also.

"We must move with haste," said Arvog, "so we may strike at Vêrmund ere he wakes."

Ilgra decided then to join the party that would retrieve the bodies. The thought of her father's remains—if remains there were—lying in an open field where the birds and beasts might pick at them bothered her more than she could say. It was a deep wrongness, one she intended to correct.

From the store of weapons, she chose a spear, and she washed the blade with her blood and named it Gorgoth, or *Revenge*.

Her mother objected, said that Ilgra was still too young. "You have not yet reached the age of the *ozhthim*, and you have not passed your trials. Wait and leave this to those who have already proven their strength."

But Ilgra rebelled. "No. I have my horns. I will not sit and cower while others venture forth."

So she broke from her mother and went to stand with Arvog's warband by the fire. They did not turn her away, but welcomed her into their fold, for their numbers were small and they needed all who were willing to help.

On the morning of the eighth day, Ilgra accompanied Arvog and the rest of the warband as they crept back to the smoldering ruins of their village. The fires had died down in the fields and the foothills, leaving the land scorched black. Many of the buildings still stood, though few without damage. Some had torn thatching, others a crushed wall or a broken beam, and everything sooty and stinking of smoke.

Finding their dead amid the devastation was no easy task. They worked in teams to sort through the rubble and scour the trampled earth, and many a grisly discovery they made. A smear of blood, a shard of bone: parts of loved ones left behind where the murderous dragon had been careless in his eating. Often it was impossible to attach a name to the parts, so Arvog had them gathered in the center of the village, and there the warband built them a proper pyre.

Ilgra labored alongside the others for half a day, silent except for when answering the occasional question or order. When last they broke to rest, she rested not but went to the wreckage of her family's hall.

There, by the pile of blistered beams, Ilgra came upon what was left of her father: a twisted, nearly unrecognizable shape, charred black by dragonfire. Grief and rage—equally strong and equally terrible—stabbed her heart, and she knelt beside him and wept.

All her life her father had protected their family. Yet at the deciding moment, when the foul worm had threatened, she had not been able to protect *him*. It was a failure Ilgra could never correct, and she knew it would haunt her all her years.

Though singed and discolored, her father's left horn was yet intact. When Ilgra could bring herself to move, she cut it from his head, chanting to the gods as she did, in the hope her prayers would smooth his way to the afterlife.

Then she gathered up his corpse and carried

it to the pyre in the center of the village. The weight of her father's body in her arms was not something that Ilgra soon forgot.

Their wretched search continued late into the evening, until they were well sure they had found every last piece of battered flesh belonging to their clanmates and placed them with grieving reverence upon the pyre. Then Ilgra and the rest of the warband performed the required rituals, and Arvog lit the tower of stacked wood.

It was a funeral fit for the bravest of warriors. And all the dead *were* warriors, even the younglings. The hated dragon had killed them in battle. They deserved the same consideration as any of the Horned who died while raiding or wrestling or otherwise attempting to win honor for their name.

As the pyre blazed bright, Arvog strode forth,

bared his throat to the great mountain Kulkaras—and to Vêrmund atop—and bellowed so loudly that his cry echoed the length of the valley. Others joined in, and Ilgra too, until they all stood facing the mountain, shouting their challenges through throats torn raw. It was a foolish, futile gesture that risked rousing the dragon's wrath, but they did not care.

The noise frightened a flock of ravens from the trees. If the sound troubled Vêrmund in his slumber, it did not show. He seemed entirely oblivious—or worse, uncaring—toward the valley below.

The warband kept vigil around the pyre while it burned, and when night fell, they made camp on the cold earth. Ilgra could not bring herself to sleep, so she stood watch beside the pillar of flames, gripping her spear and glaring at the strip of inky darkness wrapped tight around the peak of Kulkaras.

Stars still glimmered in the sky, and the first hint of grey light had just appeared above the eastern mountains when Arvog and six other warriors set out to climb Kulkaras and kill the dragon Vêrmund.

Ilgra begged to go with them, to quench her thirst for vengeance. But Arvog refused, said she was too young, too inexperienced. "We have but one chance to catch the worm unawares."

And Ilgra hated that he was right.

Then he said, "Worry not, Ilgra. With Svarvok's favor, you shall have your fill of blood today. All our clan shall."

This Ilgra accepted, but it sat badly with her. Young she was, and untested also, but the anger that burned in her belly had no match, and she felt herself equal in spirit—if not stature—with the mightiest of the Horned.

With Arvog at the lead, the seven warriors departed. Ilgra and the rest of the warband watched in silence from beside the grave of coals.

It had been agreed that midday was the best time to strike at Vêrmund. Dragons, like the great mountain cats, were known to do most of their hunting in the early mornings and late evenings. When the sun was at its highest, Vêrmund was likely to be in the deepest part of his sleep and, thus, the most vulnerable—if ever a dragon the size of Vêrmund could be described as vulnerable.

Kulkaras was a formidable mountain, and though the Horned of Clan Skgaro were strong and hardy, reaching the peak was far from easy. The way was treacherous, full of steep ascents, narrow ridges, and slopes strewn with loose rock. Rare it was any of the Skgaro sought to gain the crown of high Kulkaras unless driven by vision or honor or madness. In all Ilgra's life, only one of the clan had attempted it: a young warrior by the name of Nalvog, who had meant to prove himself by the feat when he could not prove himself by strength of arms. But Nalvog had failed in his attempt and, shamed, exiled himself from the valley. Since then, he had been seen no more.

While they waited, Ilgra and her companions sorted through the rubble for needed tools and prized possessions. The day was bleak and overcast, and rain came down upon them in fitful sweeps.

A chill crept into Ilgra's bones. She sat crouched in the lee of a feed shed and pulled her wolfskin cloak tight around her shoulders. As always, her gaze turned to Kulkaras and to Vêrmund thereupon. But no sign of Arvog or his band could she see, nor did any cry or clash reach her straining ears.

The day wore on.

Near midday, one of Ilgra's companions, Yarzhek, claimed to hear a sound from the mountaintop: a crack or a shout of some kind. But none of the others in the ruined village heard it, and Ilgra was doubtful. Soon after, she spotted what appeared to be a puff of smoke rising from Kulkaras, but after studying it, she decided the haze was actually a scrap of windblown cloud.

As the sun started toward the jagged horizon, it seemed clear that Arvog's group had either been delayed in their purpose or had failed entirely.

Dispirited, Ilgra and the others gathered around the remnants of the pyre. There they sat, hunched and unspeaking, while dusk settled over the valley.

The hollow moon had just peeked over the mountains when they heard footsteps approaching. Down the path to Kulkaras came four of the seven who had departed. All were smeared with dirt and blood, and they appeared heartsick, footsore, and hungry. Arvog and another of the

Anointed carried one of the Skgaro, who looked to have a broken ankle, while Arvog himself bore a deep gash above his brow.

Ilgra approved of the gash. It served his features well. "What happened?" she asked.

Setting down their injured companion, Arvog answered: "The dragon heard us. Heard or smelled, I know not which, but when we drew near, he lifted his tail and dropped it upon us. The four of us barely escaped being crushed. The others . . ." He shook his head. "We could not reach their bodies."

Then Ilgra bent her neck with sorrow, mourning their deaths. She hoped their spirits might someday find safe passage to the afterlife.

What remained of the warband was somber indeed as they started back through the dark and the rain. When they arrived at the hall of Zhar, Arvog gave the clan a full accounting of their expedition, and the Herndall decided: they would not trouble Vêrmund the Grim again, not until or unless they had a better plan for ridding themselves of the cunning old worm.

Ilgra hated the decision, but having no suggestion of her own, she held her tongue.

The oldest of the Herndall, Elgha Nine-Fingers, then said, "We are fortunate you did not anger Vêrmund such that he came seeking after us. But we should not rest easy. Dragons have long memories and are slow to forgive. It is known."

And all agreed.

Later still, when she sat with her mother and sister, Ilgra showed them the horn she had cut from her father's head. As eldest heir, the horn was hers to keep, but Yhana touched it and said, "I am glad you did this." And Ilgra saw tears in her eyes, and she knew then the measure of her sister's grief, and it was no less than her own.

Days passed. In that time, the clan did their best to ignore the dragon perched atop Kulkaras. Instead, they tracked and captured the livestock that had survived the attack. They saved what seeds and materials they could. And one by one, those of the Skgaro who still had halls intact enough to ward off the weather began to return to the village.

Ilgra's father had been a good hunter, and a Speaker of Truths for the Anointed—a position of no small importance. With him now gone, and their home destroyed, Ilgra and her family had no choice but to take refuge in the hall of Barzhqa, brother to her mother and much like her in make and temperament.

It rankled Ilgra that they needed to depend on Barzhqa's generosity. But their choices were limited, and they were lucky not to be stuck living with Zhar, who always smelled of fish.

In the evenings, when she was free, Ilgra took her father's horn to a stream and soaked it in the swift-flowing current. When the marrow of the horn was soft, she scraped it out and smoothed the inside with heated stones until it was slick as shell. Then she gave the horn to Darvek, and he carved a mouthpiece from the thigh bone of a bear, scribed the woven pattern of their family history around the belled end, and last of all, knotted a leather carrying strap round the middle.

When it was finished, an expanse of wonder broadened Ilgra's heart. She put her lips to the mouthpiece and sounded the horn with a mighty breath. A brazen note rang forth, loud and deep-throated—a challenge to all who might oppose her. In it, Ilgra heard an echo of her father's voice, and a sorrowful joy filled her eyes with tears.

A fortnight after Vêrmund's bloody reaving, a

wandering shaman came to them from the south.
The shaman was short but thick in every measure, and his horns curled twice around his ears.
His name was Ulkrö, and he carried a staff cut
with runes and with a single sapphire, large as his
thumb, set within the knotted wood. He claimed
to have heard of Vêrmund and said that he, Ulkrö,
could kill the dragon.

Ilgra listened with resentment: if anyone were
to kill Vêrmund the Grim, it ought to be her. But
it was a selfish desire, so she spoke of it not. The
shaman frightened her: he passed his staff through
the hall fire and made the flames dance at his
command. She did not understand magic. She
put her trust in bone and muscle, not words and
potions.

The next morning, Ulkrö set forth to climb
Kulkaras and confront the dragon. The whole
clan turned out to watch, a silent gathering of
hard-eyed faces, too wracked with sorrow to cheer

or hope. Ulkrö made up for their quiet with japes and gibes and shows of magic. He finished with a bolt of lightning from his staff, with which he split a sapling, sending it tumbling to the ground. At that, the clan broke their stillness and gave full voice to a war chant as the shaman made his departure.

That evening, when the sun streamed low across the mountain peaks and the valley lay in purple shadow, Ilgra heard a roar from Vêrmund. Fear struck through her, and she and her family rushed outside, as did the rest of Clan Skgaro.

Upon high Kulkaras, they saw the giant worm spread his coal-black wings and rise up rampant before the amber sky. His head was wreathed with flashes of light, and fire burst from his maw, an angry banner that rippled as if in a beating gale. Shadows clung round the dragon, unnatural in the extreme, and slabs of stone split off the face of Kulkaras and fell to shatter against the trees below.

Whatever else could be said of the shaman Ulkrö, he was neither coward nor weakling, and his magics served him well. For a fraught span, the battle raged fierce and ferocious. Then the hollow shriek of the deathbird sounded among the trees, and a flare of red light went up from Kulkaras— a great beacon bright enough to pierce the gathered clouds and breach the heavens beyond. A moment later, the light vanished. They heard Vêrmund utter a triumphant bellow, and then all was still and all was quiet.

At dawn's first light, Ilgra crept out with the warriors, fearful to see what Ulkrö had wrought. They turned their gazes northward, and there upon the peak of Kulkaras the scaled length of Vêrmund again coiled around the jagged rock, seemingly unperturbed by the night's events.

Ilgra felt the grey leach of hopelessness, and she looked at Gorgoth, her spear, and wondered what hope *she* had of ever defeating the dragon Vêrmund. It was not in her nature to give up, though. Ilgra was her father's daughter. By his name, she swore she would have her vengeance.

▽ ▽ ▽

Two things Ulkrö had proven by his attack: First, that Vêrmund was content to stay on Kulkaras and sleep off his meal. Second, that the dragon was no more vulnerable to magic than he was to swords, spears, axes, or arrows.

It was a disheartening realization for the Skgaro. There was talk of making weighted nets big enough to snare Vêrmund's wings, but the season was turning from summer to autumn, and much needed doing were they to survive the harsh mountain winter.

So the Skgaro put aside their plans for killing the dragon, and though they knew it was a risk, they began the task of rebuilding their village. They built more with stone than wood this time, and it was a tiresome labor for the males, who preferred hunting or raiding or sparring among themselves to determine who was strongest. But they prevailed, and their halls rose anew.

The Skgaro also dug hidden burrows throughout the foothills and stocked them well with provisions. It went against every fiber of their being to contemplate hiding like prey—the Horned bow to nothing and no one—but necessity forced them to it. The younglings had to survive, and the seedstock for next year's planting too.

And they set watch upon Kulkaras at all times, night and day. Should Vêrmund descend again, they would have warning.

Many watches Ilgra stood. When not at her post—nor hewing stone or weeding their meager crops or tending flocks or any of the myriad tasks required of her—she devoted herself to working with her spear and learning from Arvog and the other warriors how best to fight. It was custom among the Horned for both males and females to train in the use of weapons—for theirs was a war-like people—but Ilgra pursued the practice with greater enthusiasm than most. She forsook the arts of hearth and home, much to her mother's disapproval, and spent herself in contest with the males until she could hold her own with all but the strongest.

Thus the year crept past. With help from their clanmates, Ilgra and her family finished their new hall, and thereupon they set to making it a fit place to live ere the weather turned cold. And still Vêrmund remained perched upon Kulkaras, lost in his gluttonous slumber. At times, they heard rumblings from the mountain as the worm shifted or as he snored, knocking loose falls of ice and snow, and there were nights when fire lit the undersides of the clouds as Vêrmund exhaled particularly forcefully.

Inevitably, the younger males began to seek to earn a name for themselves by climbing Kulkaras and marking a spur of rock close to the dragon without waking him. The Herndall disapproved of the practice, but their disapproval did nothing to stop it.

At first the recklessness of the climbs bothered Ilgra. But then she decided they were a help to her, for they served to accustom Vêrmund to the occasional visitor—if indeed he even noticed. The accounts of those who reached the summit of Kulkaras also helped give her a sense of how she might accomplish the same. She listened with starved interest to each warrior upon his return, and in her mind, she pictured the path, imagined sneaking up on the sleeping worm. . . .

The nearest any of the males got was within

a stone's throw of Vêrmund's wing. It was impossible to cross the final stretch of scree-strewn granite without making noise, and none of the Horned, not even the most boastful, were willing to attempt it.

As for herself, Ilgra would not risk climbing Kulkaras unless she felt sure of being able to kill grim Vêrmund. So she held and waited.

The peace could not last, though. The whole clan knew it, and they lived with the knowledge of impending doom, and it wore upon them.

▽　　▽　　▽

At first snowfall their nightmares came true: Vêrmund woke and, with a fearsome cry, unfurled his wings and took to the air. He wheeled in lazy circles above the gleaming spire of Kulkaras and then drifted down with the sound of rushing wind.

The clan fled. Ilgra too, clutching Yhana in one hand and Gorgoth in the other, while their mother hurried to keep up. They scattered to their burrows and sat huddled there while the dragon prowled among their halls and holdings. This time, no one tried to attack Vêrmund; the males cursed and brandished their weapons, but they dared not break cover.

The scaly old worm crept through the valley, dining upon deer and sheep and all manner of animals. However, he ate little compared with before and set only one small fire in the fields by the streams.

Then Vêrmund licked his chops with a tongue that was barbed like that of a cat. Seemingly satisfied, he returned to the air and, after several more lazy circles, settled once again on Kulkaras. He released a single huff of smoke, tucked his snout under his tail, and closed his crimson eyes.

Unbelieving, Ilgra crawled out of her burrow.

None of the clan had been hurt, and the animals they had lost were not enough to starve them.

The Herndall consulted, and then Elgha nodded and said, "This we can endure."

And so it was. Enduring was not to Ilgra's taste, nor to any of the Skgaro's, but it was better than being eaten.

Winter aged into spring, spring into summer, and then summer again to winter. The clan hunted and farmed and mated, and once more grew strong. Far above, Vêrmund was a black blight upon the crown of Kulkaras, a looming menace often seen and often spoken of but rarely an immediate threat. As they grew accustomed to his presence, the Skgaro came to view Vêrmund as more a part of the landscape than a living creature. To them he was no different from a force of nature: a blizzard or a plague that might strike without warning and that, for the most part, was best ignored.

If asked, the Skgaro would claim they still wished to kill the dragon, and in evenings, they often twisted cord for the much-discussed nets. But the yardage needed was far more than they could make in any reasonable period of time, and the nets remained unrealized.

True it was, Vêrmund sometimes roused himself and came flying down amid fire and fury to steal from their herds, and if any of the clan were foolish enough to challenge him, the dragon would eat them too. Yet Vêrmund's attacks were not the most important part of their lives. Wood still needed chopping. Livestock still needed guarding against wolves and bears and sharp-eyed mountain cats. Crops still needed tending. The daily duties necessary to survival took precedence.

And Ilgra hated it. Complacency rankled her to no end; her blood called for vengeance, and every moment of delay was a frustration. Worse, there were some within the clan who began to speak of Vêrmund in reverent tones, as if *he* were worthy of respect. Several times, while herding flocks from one pasture to the next, Ilgra found small shrines in the foothills of Kulkaras, shrines with offerings of food and drink meant for the devouring worm. She destroyed them all. Had she known who built them, she would have beaten them with Gorgoth until they were bruised from head to heel.

Ilgra kept at her training, and her strength and skill continued to grow. Sparring with Arvog was no preparation for fighting the dragon, but because of it, she felt increasingly confident in her abilities.

The day of her *ozhthim* came late that winter, and upon its coming, the trials of passage, wherein Ilgra had to stand before the whole of the clan and prove her courage. Despite her fear, she held her place, and reaching the end, the dams marked her as a full member of Clan Skgaro.

But the trials were very hard. They were supposed to be. It was seven days before Ilgra was recovered enough to leave her hall, and three moons after that before the wounds on her chest had healed. Ilgra wore the scars as the badge of honor they were, and she wished her father had been there to see, for she knew he would have been proud. Not once had she cried out during the whole ordeal. Not once.

With the trials complete and her skills with Gorgoth well advanced, Ilgra finally felt ready to pair action with intent. Yet she bided her time a while longer, until winter broke and most of the snowy cap melted off high Kulkaras's brow. Then one evening, when the air was mild and the fields were green, she filled a pouch with unguent for burns and with berries and cheese and dried strips of meat. She sharpened Gorgoth once more—so it could cut a strand of hair with the lightest touch—and she brushed and cleaned her leather armor, oiled it so it gleamed by the hall fire.

She said nothing of her plans to her mother or sister, only kissed each on the forehead before retiring to bed.

When the birds first sounded in the grey before dawn, Ilgra rose and slipped from the hall and, in the coolness of morning, turned to face Kulkaras.

None marked her passing as she snuck through the village, not even Razhag, the male on watch. When she reached the forest edge, Ilgra quickened her pace, heading toward the ridge of earth and stone that would allow her to climb Kulkaras's flank. It was the same path the shaman Ulkrö had followed, and the knowledge gave her a moment of pause.

Still, an expanding sense of excitement filled Ilgra's heart, and she moved forward with light steps, glad to at last be taking action.

Despite Ulkrö's failure, and that of Arvog's warband before, Ilgra felt sure she could succeed where they had failed. The reasons for her confidence were simple: she was not going to attempt to match Vêrmund in open combat. (Though Ilgra was willing to risk her life in pursuit of vengeance, she was not willing to throw it away in a hopeless gambit.) And she had become convinced that Arvog's warband had failed in their quest because of the noise the seven warriors had made on the rock face. The lone males who had ascended Kulkaras had managed to avoid attracting Vêrmund's attention. Thuswise, Ilgra felt she could do the same. By herself, she could be quiet in a way no group of Horned could, and she had other means of avoiding detection besides. . . .

Then it would just be a matter of a quick thrust of Gorgoth beneath Vêrmund's armored eyelid, and the dragon would die. The thrust would need to be long to reach the worm's brain, but Ilgra had no doubt that—with the memory of her father guiding her arm—she could hit her mark.

When she came upon a small stream that poured out of the ground and down a mossy gully, she stopped to fill her skins. As she held them beneath the icy water, she breathed deep, enjoying the smell of the stream and the peaceful sound of water burbling over wood and stone. For she knew it might be the last time she would savor such a simple pleasure.

Onward she forged, through brake and bramble, up rise and ridge, across saddle and scarp, until the village was a shrunken cluster below, as tiny as a youngling's toys. Often outcroppings of rock blocked the way, and Ilgra had to climb from one precarious hold to another, knowing that if her hands slipped, she might lose her life. The sun beat hot throughout the day, and sweat gathered upon her brow and dripped into her eyes so they stung. She ate while walking, but sparingly, not wanting her stomach to be heavy with food.

So steep was Kulkaras that, for most of the ascent, the mountain hid the bulk of Vêrmund from her sight. She could hear the dragon, though, snorting and growling in his sleep, and when he shifted his weight, the bones of the mountain groaned and birds flew in fright from the boughs of the trees.

Eventually and inevitably, Vêrmund came into sight. First a section of his tail, extending over the side of Kulkaras like a great black cliff, sharp and jagged. Then a fold of wing, thicker than any hide and laced with pulsing veins the width of her legs. And last of all, the huge white claws of one forefoot—curved, saw-toothed, and cruelly pointed—and above, the dragon's wedge-shaped head, partially covered by a length of tail.

A heavy odor clung to the worm, a sour musk that reminded her of the den of a large cat. It was a warning scent, the scent of an eater of flesh.

Ilgra stopped at the first, distant glimpse of Vêrmund and made her final preparations. She tied rags around her feet that they might not betray her with unwanted sound. And she poured water onto the sparse earth and smeared herself with mud to hide her own scent. Were she hunting deer, she would have used pine needles or chokeweed, but so high on the mountain only moss and lichen grew. She finished by rubbing her skin with a mat of wool she had hung over the hearth in their hall, so as to gather the scent of smoke. The worm so often spouted smoke from his nostrils, she felt sure he had long since ceased to smell it.

Then Ilgra gathered her courage and resumed her climb, only slower and more careful than before.

When some time later she gained a clear

view of Vêrmund's head, she froze, and her heart redoubled in pace. For she saw a slit of red in Vêrmund's eye, and she realized he slept with the armored lid partially open. She studied the mountaintop: the stone was rotten and split in heavy slabs. Deep scratches scored the surface, and scales big as both her hands lay scattered among the pieces of scree, while patches of un-melted snow filled the shadowed hollows. Near the dragon's folded wing, Ilgra spotted the flat-faced boulder marked with the sigils of those war-riors who had reached the summit.

Careful not to disturb the loose-strewn rock, Ilgra edged around the dragon, always keeping a slab of stone between her and the crimson eye. If she could get close enough, she could strike before the worm had a chance to react. Even if she failed in killing him, she would still half blind him, and he would be disadvantaged forevermore.

She whispered a prayer to her father and to

Rahna, queen of the gods, and by them she bolstered her courage.

The thinness of the air made her want to gasp. The strength of her anticipation sped her pulse. Every muscle in her body was strung taut in readiness for action. Tremors of nervous excitement wracked her steps. Already she could feel the frenzy of battle rage—the great boon and bane of her people—rising within her, and she bared her teeth with feral glee.

Near an hour passed before Ilgra finally maneuvered herself behind a slab within striking distance of Vêrmund's enormous head. She stayed crouched there while she calmed her breathing and readied her spirit. Should she die, it would be a glorious death, and the clan would sing her name for generations to come. She touched the horn of her father, where it hung on her hip. She wished she could wind it, but she dared not

lose the advantage of surprise. Every chance of
success rested upon it.

Ilgra took a breath. Then she vaulted over the
slab and ran headlong toward the dragon, spear
held high. Three quick steps, and she drove her
weapon toward the narrow slit of Vêrmund's sleeping eye.

The dragon blinked.

With a loud *ping*, the blade of the spear shattered against Vêrmund's scaled lid, and the haft
bounced back in Ilgra's hands, numbing her palms.
She stumbled to a stop. For a brief moment, she
stood motionless, dumbfounded.

The lid lifted. A blazing, red-rimmed eye
stared down at her, the pupil a black crevice large
enough to walk through. The eye filled the sky;
it dominated her existence, pinning her in place
with palpable force. Then the dragon's mind en-
veloped her own, and Ilgra shrank before the vast

and incomprehensible nature of its intelligence. From it she felt not surprise, nor anger, nor even amusement, but the worst of all reactions . . . indifference.

Her sense of self faltered beneath the withering onslaught of Vêrmund's presence. The world seemed to tilt around her, and darkness yawned wide with a hungry grin, and all she knew and all she was became no more important than a mote of dust, adrift in an endless void. . . .

Fury freed Ilgra of the dragon's dangerous hold, and she reached for her father's horn as she backed away. She could endure many things from the worm, but not indifference. Never that! If it was the last thing she did, she would shake Vêrmund from his apathy and force him to respond as was proper, force him to *respect* her. That much she—and her clan—was owed.

Ilgra lifted the horn to her lips, about to give voice to her outrage, when the scree betrayed her.

Her foot slipped on a loose piece of rock, and she fell tumbling backward off the barren ridge atop proud Kulkaras.

She flailed and lost her grip on Gorgoth. Finding no purchase, she pulled the horn against her belly, holding it close as sky and mountain spun in a dizzying circle. Icy snow broke against her, and then brush and branches, until—with a jolt so violent her vision flashed white and a spangle of stars obscured her sight—Ilgra fetched up against the twisted trunk of a wind-warped fir.

Like all the Horned, Ilgra had a thick skin, as thick as that of a winter boar. It protected her from many wounds, but it could not protect her from the worst. When her breath returned in sudden gasps and she strove to move, Ilgra discovered her leg was broken, and she cried out with pain.

Her spear was nowhere to be seen.

She lay there for a hopeless while, staring

toward the peak, waiting for Vêrmund to crawl down the face of Kulkaras and devour her. She could neither run nor fight nor hide, so Ilgra did what was only sensible and held still to conserve her strength.

But Vêrmund never appeared. It seemed she was entirely unimportant so far as the dragon was concerned. The realization aggravated Ilgra nearly as much as her broken leg; it wasn't right the worm should have so much power over their lives—the very power of life and death—and yet to him, they were no more than scurrying mice.

Ilgra snarled and pulled herself upright, though the effort nearly caused her to again cry out. She clung to the tree, as a drowning swimmer clings to the slightest hold, and waited while the torment of her leg slowly subsided. She checked her father's horn, the strap still knotted round her fist, and was gladdened to see it well and whole.

As Ilgra readied to move, she spotted a glint of brilliant blue in the nearby scrub. Curious, she dropped to hands and knees and crawled closer, each touch of leg to ground sending a lance of pain through her body. She parted the scrub with her hands, and there, among the knotted stems, saw the staff of Ulkrö the shaman.

Wonder overcame her, for the wood appeared untouched by the mountain's harsh clime. Ilgra took the staff then, and as she held it before her, she decided: if she could not best Vêrmund by strength of limb, she would have to best him with less honest means—with spells and spirits and the twisting of words. The thought frightened her, but Ilgra had never been one to let fear win out.

Then she named the staff as she had named her spear: Gorgoth, or *Revenge*.

She crawled back to the fir, cut a branch, and with a strip torn from her tunic, bound it to her broken leg. Then, using the staff as a crutch, she began the long climb back down Kulkaras to the valley floor.

It was a miserable ordeal. Every step hurt, and ere long Ilgra's throat grew dry and the ache of hunger hollowed out her stomach, for she had lost her food and water in the fall.

She stopped often to rest her leg, and it was deep into the gloaming when the orange light of the first hall appeared twinkling between the branches of the trees. A welcome sight, for it promised warmth and safety and good food.

Arvog and Moqtar found her before she reached the hall. They greeted her with cries of relief and looked with wonder at the staff she bore. The two had been waiting for her since morn. As Arvog explained, when it became known she had departed, it took but a short while before they found her spoor and tracked her to the base of Kulkaras. None dared follow past that point, for fear of what Vêrmund might do if she roused the dragon. But they had kept watch, in hope she would return.

"Your mother is much worried," said Arvog in his low rumble. Ilgra nodded. She had expected nothing else.

They carried her back home. There her mother and sister descended upon Ilgra with a concern fierce enough to give even Vêrmund—evil as he was—pause. And yet Ilgra could tell, despite the cuffs and accusations, that her mother was proud: what Ilgra had done was a feat equal to those of the bravest warriors. And while she had not suc-ceeded in killing the dragon, she had retrieved a great treasure in Ulkrö's staff.

Yhana too seemed proud, and she said, "Were I grown into my horns, I would have gone with you, Ilgra-sister. You did what I cannot yet do, and for that I am glad."

Then her mother said, "You are finished now,

yes? You have satisfied the demands of honor. You will not attempt any more foolishness."

But Ilgra's discontent remained. So long as Vêrmund lived, she could not rest easy. Only the blood of the dragon could slake her thirst for vengeance. She made to say as much, but the arrival of the healer ended the conversation.

A leather belt was fit between Ilgra's teeth, and she bit down while the bone in her leg was pulled straight and set. She made no sound but stared at the ceiling and thought of the staff and all she needed to learn. For Ilgra was young and yet undaunted.

▽ ▽ ▽

Her leg healed badly. She had further damaged it during her descent from Kulkaras, and the bone knit with a bend so that, forever after, she walked with a limp, as the one leg was shorter than the other. It hurt too, in damp and cold and after walks, but Ilgra never let the discomfort prevent her from going where she wanted.

One thing was certain, however: her days as a warrior had reached their end. Her balance was poor, and if some foe struck her crippled leg, it would give way and was like to break again.

The knowledge was a bitter drop upon her tongue. Ilgra found her thoughts wandering down unaccustomed paths, dark and tangled. At times she would remember the feel of Vêrmund's mind, and then the world seemed to grow dim and distant and she would have to sit until the sensation passed.

Despite her leg, Ilgra grew ever taller. By autumn it was clear she was Anointed, as was her father before, and one by one, the males came courting. Those she could not ignore, she beat about the head and shoulders with Gorgoth and so chased them away. For the clan feared the staff and the magics it contained.

Her mother and sister disapproved, but Ilgra had no desire to take a mate. Such would only distract from her larger goal. She said nothing of her intent, though, and merely claimed no male had done enough to win her favor. That was, for the moment, enough to quell their concern.

What time she had of her own, Ilgra spent in study with the staff, attempting to learn its secrets, but her efforts bore no fruit; she knew not the ways of weirding, and whatever powers the staff possessed—set there by Ulkrö himself—remained a mystery.

Her lack of progress became an ever-greater source of discontent; Ilgra could hardly sleep at nights for thinking about the riddle the staff presented. At last, late in the season, she decided her only hope of success lay in seeking out a mentor who might instruct her in magic. The thought of leaving the valley pained her greatly, but doing nothing was a still greater torment.

For once, fortune smiled upon her. Just as Ilgra began her preparations, another shaman arrived at the village, and his name was Qarzhad Stone-Fist. To him Ilgra showed the staff and confessed her desire to learn the weirding arts, but Qarzhad scoffed and made claim on the staff by right of his chosen craft.

Ilgra laughed at his claim, and the clan laughed with her. No outlander could tell the Skgaro what spoils were theirs to keep, not even a shaman. Then Qarzhad locked horns with her, and laughter turned to threats, and it was only with much wrestling and shouting that they reached a compromise that dissatisfied them both—this being the hallmark of all good compromises. What they settled upon was a wager: a full round of Maghra, three games of three. Should Ilgra win, Qarzhad would take her as apprentice and teach her his secret knowledge. And should Qarzhad win, Ilgra would surrender the staff and that would be the end of the matter.

Though surprised by Ilgra's challenge, her mother did not object. To be a shaman was to be a person of importance. It would bring honor to their family. Moreover, any clan lucky enough to have a spellweaver of their own was all but guaranteed to survive the winter.

The contest was held that evening. The whole village gathered in Arvog's hall to watch. Ilgra and Qarzhad sat with lowered horns, one across from the other and the polished table of bone between.

Nine games in total they played, nine as was the sacred number. Ilgra won *Beater*, the first set of three, and Qarzhad won *Biter*, the second set. This was no more than Ilgra had expected. When it came to *Breaker*, the third and final set, Ilgra knew she had the upper horn. *Breaker* could be

won either by attacking your opponent or by flee-
ing before them and so catching them in a trap
of your own making. Like most warriors, Qarzhad
was too proud to flee, but for herself, Ilgra no
longer had any pride. She only cared to win. So
she broke, and by breaking, won.

Qarzhad cursed her, but a wager was a wager,
and he to his pledged word was true.

At morn's first light, Ilgra met the shaman in
an empty meadow along the shadowed edge of
the forest, and there it was she began her apprenticeship.

▽   ▽   ▽

For three moons Ilgra labored under the instruction
of Qarzhad. He was a cruel and uncompromising
tutor, but Ilgra minded not. She wanted to learn,
and she was willing to drive herself far beyond the
bounds of comfort.

And learn she did. Qarzhad taught her the rules of weirding and of the ancient language used to reshape the world according to one's will. He showed Ilgra how to govern her thoughts and feelings, and how to touch the minds of others, even as Vêrmund had done with hers. When by herself, Ilgra strove to memorize the names and words Qarzhad saw fit to share with her: words of power that spoke to the true nature of things.

Her mother, and the clan as a whole, freed Ilgra of all but the most basic responsibilities so she could devote herself to study. She did not tell them of her greater goal, though—not even her family—preferring to keep it clasped close to her heart.

At the end of the three moons, Qarzhad Stone-Fist departed. He was at heart a wanderer, and there were other clans—clans without shamans— that needed his services. Ere he left, he gave Ilgra a list of tasks: skills to master, words to practice, tools to make. Also too a list of prohibitions: things she was *not* to do—foremost of which was any weirding that broke the laws of nature, and second any weirding with Ulkrö's staff.

While he was gone, Ilgra was consistent with her practice. She strove to excel that she might surprise Qarzhad upon his return and so she might accomplish her greater goal all the sooner. For the longest time, Ilgra felt as if she were butting her head against stone: nothing about weirding came easily. But she persisted, and just as horn grows too slowly to notice from day to day and yet after a span of months the changes are plain to see, so too did Ilgra's understanding progress.

The weirding felt strange to Ilgra. She was ill accustomed to using word or thought to force a change. At first it seemed a cheat, but the weirding exacted a price of effort in proportion to the ambition of her intent, and the price comforted Ilgra, assured her that she was still a member of the Horned and not a spirit or a god. She was still bound to the earth and the trees and the reality of life itself.

Qarzhad returned at the end of harvest, and Ilgra showed him all she had accomplished. If the shaman was impressed, he did not say, only worked her harder, gave her more tasks—ones that forced her well past the limits of her abilities.

Again, Qarzhad stayed some few moons, and then again he left to resume his wandering. In like manner, Ilgra's apprenticeship continued.

As moons gathered into seasons, and then seasons into years, Ilgra learned many things: she learned the true names of the deer and the bears and all the birds and beasts of the mountains. Also too the plants, be they ever so large or small. And she learned how to speak to the wind and the earth and the flames of the fire and how to coax them into doing her bidding. The riddle of steel

became hers and the secrets of binding and ward-
ing and making.

In time, Qarzhad taught her the truth about her
staff—no longer Ulkrö's, now *hers*. The sapphire
set within the end contained a great storehouse of
power that broke and battered like a wildling sea
against its sharp-edged prison. Should that prison
fail, the sea would rush forth in a torrent and destroy all who were near. But if the shaman who
wielded the staff were wise, they could harness the
power to their will and use it to accomplish great
feats—feats that one person alone could not hope
to otherwise accomplish. The power was not to be
squandered, though. It was a treasure more valu-
able than the stone itself: a gleaming hoard that
Ulkrö and his master before him had gathered
over the course of their lifetimes. The power was
to be husbanded against moments of rare need,
and between those, Ilgra should add to it herself,

nurture it, feed it with the strength of her body so the hoard might grow to even greater size and she might pass it on in turn.

And Ilgra understood: the power was a legacy. But she had no intention of preserving it, and for that, she felt guilty.

Twice she accompanied Qarzhad on his wanderings. She had never left the valley of the Skgaro before, and the sight of new mountains both excited and unsettled her, and the clans they visited had unfamiliar customs that ofttimes made her feel less than hearth-welcome. Still, the travel was useful, and she was grateful for the experiences, for they revealed to her the true size of the world. More than that, they strengthened her love and appreciation of home. The valley contained every good thing a clan needed: clean water, plentiful game, trees and stone for building. The only fault it had was Vêrmund; if she could but remove him, their home would again be as it should.

In those years, Vêrmund's lengths of slumber were unpredictable, but the clan grew familiar with his attacks, and of them, few surprises came. As long as they kept their distance and angered not the worm, they could expect to survive. There were exceptions—accidents on their part, sometimes malice on Vêrmund's—but the exceptions were rare enough to bear.

None of which Ilgra could accept with any good grace, and Vêrmund's presence remained a hard lump stuck in her throat.

Then one day a neighboring clan, the Clan Ynvek, came raiding.

It happened in late summer, when the fields were full and the animals fattened. The Ynvek surprised them at the height of the midday sun. With whoops and bellows and wild cries, the Ynvek's warriors charged out of the forest, shaking spears and hammers and poles with woven pennants displaying family crests.

Such raids were common among the clans. They were a good way for males to test themselves and win a name sufficient to attract a mate. For the most part, the raids were, while not entirely friendly, not entirely hostile. Blood would be shed, but rare it was that a member of either clan lost their life.

In this case, a raid upon the Skgaro would be considered an opportunity to capture an outsized share of glory, seeing as how they lived beneath the shadow of a dragon. Already their clan had acquired a reputation for bravery far beyond the norm.

So it was that, when the raid occurred, Ilgra deemed it more an exciting distraction than a serious threat. She ran from her family's rebuilt hall and joined the clan in beating back the intruders. As always, the males took the lead, but it was a group effort: all but the younglings were honor-bound to participate. Even the oldest of the Herndall took up arms (mainly canes and reed brooms, which stung like hornets).

While Ilgra shook her staff at a bewildered Ynvek, she watched with admiration as Arvog grappled with the largest of the attacking warriors and beat him to the ground. Then another Ynvek charged over and tried to seize her—she was Anointed, after all, and much prized on that account—and Ilgra struck him with Gorgoth, and with a weirding word set swampfire on the tips of his horns. The greenish flames held no heat, but the Ynvek shrieked a most unseemly sound and fled, panic-struck, toward the nearest stream, batting at his burning horns the whole while.

And Ilgra was much amused.

The sounds of their contest rang loud in the noonday air: the clanging of wood and iron, the bellows and shouts of the males, the curses and exhortations of the females, and the outraged bleating of the livestock.

The clamor was loud enough, it seemed, that it reached all the way to the lofty peak of high Kulkaras. For amid their fighting, Ilgra heard a warning shout, and she turned to see Vêrmund the Grim lifting his head from its stony pillow.

The dragon peered toward the valley floor, and their fighting ceased as Vêrmund uttered a rolling, rumbling, avalanche-inducing growl. The growl was so powerful, Ilgra felt it in her feet and in her bones. The surface of the ground blurred with vibration. Animals cowered, streams rippled, and the air darkened as flocks of screaming birds fled the forest. Atop Kulkaras, slabs of ice and snow cleaved from the granite peak and fell with soft thunder into the ranks of trees below, snapping their hoary trunks like stalks of dry straw.

The worm's meaning could not have been any clearer.

Then Vêrmund lowered his head, closed his eyes, and appeared to sink back into sleep.

The Ynvek paled and put away their weapons. Without another word, they fled back whence they came, taking with them neither mates nor livestock nor trophies nor glory itself.

And Ilgra crossed her arms and glared at the distant dragon. That he felt possessive of his private foodstocks did nothing to lessen her hate.

▽　▽　▽

After four full years of instruction, Qarzhad Stone-Fist announced that there was nothing more he could teach her. Indeed, Ilgra had already surpassed him in mastery of weirding. But as he cautioned her, mastery did not always imply wisdom.

Ilgra thanked him, for she was grateful for his tutelage and she had grown fond of the ill-tempered shaman over the years.

Then Qarzhad took her by the horns and said, "I know the ambition that lies in your heart, Ilgra

213

Lamefoot. Well I understand it. Once I had a mate, a strong, fierce Horned not unlike yourself. But one spring, she chanced upon a bear that had woken from its winter slumber. It was mean and hungry, and it attacked her. I found her, still alive, but all my years of study, all my skill and knowledge, were not enough to save her."

"Is that why you wander?" Ilgra asked.

Qarzhad nodded, and still he held her horns. "The bear was a lone male, without a territory of its own. I set out to track it and kill it, but never did I find it, and since that day, more than a score of years has now passed."

"Then why not return home?"

The shaman smiled. It was the first true smile she had seen of him. "Because there are others in the world who need helping, and to help is a great good and a better use of my life. It is not the way of our people, Ilgra, but my counsel is this: abandon your quest for vengeance ere it destroys you. The dragon outstrips us all. You are strong and clever, and you care for our kind. It would be a sorrow to lose you to a rash adventure that kills so many of our young warriors."

Ilgra was silent as she thought upon his words. Then she said, "Your counsel means much to me, Qarzhad, and I thank you for it, but I cannot forget my father, and I cannot abandon my quest."

"Did I say you should forget? . . . I shall not argue with you on this, Ilgra. Only think well on what you do. You have been a good apprentice of mine. No matter your chosen path, you have my blessing. May the gods grant you good fortune, and may you always be of sharp mind and clear conscience."

Then Qarzhad released her horns and once more departed. And Ilgra knew he would not soon return.

Now confident of her abilities, Ilgra set to work with eager desire. For she had a plan: the dragon was a creature of fire, and if that fire could be extinguished, then might Vêrmund be killed. And how best to snuff out a fire but with the cleansing force of water?

For three days she walked the valley fringe, searching for the place that might best serve her. All dissatisfied her until—at last—she thought of the pool where she used to swim, the selfsame pool where she had watched Vêrmund's dread arrival.

The pool itself was too small for her purpose, but the overspill poured into a deep and winding ravine with walls of stone, moisture blackened and green-spotted with mosses, lichens, and hanging tendrils that put forth pale flowers in spring's early days. If the ravine were blocked at its narrowest point, a great store of water would build up behind the blockage—and should that store break loose, woe betide any caught in the water's path. They would be trapped between the stony walls, beaten and bashed and battered beyond saving.

It was a thought most pleasing.

Yet still Ilgra kept her plans to herself. Although uncertain of their success, she saw no merit in debate or discussion. Nothing could turn her aside from her chosen path. Besides, the outrush of water would pose little danger to the Skgaro; the ravine and the stream sat some distance south of their village and, like the other streams nestled among the folds of the mountains, fed into the Hralloq River that ran north to south along the valley floor, from conquered Kulkaras to distant, saw-toothed Ulvarvek that marked the limit of the clan's holdings.

But there were problems to be solved. How to build the blockage. And once it was built, how best to lure Vêrmund the Grim into the ravine. In autumn, the clan would trap geese by digging narrow, sloping trenches that they baited with suet. The geese would follow the bait, unsuspecting, and find themselves caught in the deep end of the trenches, unable to spread their wings and fly. . . . Goose or dragon, the principle was the same.

Ilgra wasted no time in putting plan to action.

First she left her family's hall and raised herself a small hut on the crest of the ravine. This occasioned much argument with her mother, who felt it wrong of Ilgra to remove herself from the daily doings of the village. "It is not good," she said. "Not for you and not for us."

But Ilgra insisted, and her departure became a festering sore between them. As for the rest of the Skgaro, they accepted Ilgra's removal without question. The weavers of spells were seen as separate from the normal strand of the Horned, and strangeness of behavior was expected of them.

Once ensconced in her hut, alone with the wind and the howls of wandering wolves, Ilgra began her work. Speaking words of power, she carved a path through the dirt and thus diverted the overspill from the spring-fed pool into a channel alongside the lip of the ravine. With the stream coursing along a new path, she was then free to descend into the rocky cleft below without having to contend with the flow of water.

All that summer and autumn, Ilgra labored to dam up the ravine at the point where the stone walls stood closest: a pinched gap no wider than twice the full span of her arms. Though her leg was not fit for fighting, she was Anointed and, like all Anointed, strong. She toiled mightily, and by dint of her efforts, filled the gap with boulders carried from high on the mountain's side.

As each boulder dropped into place, Ilgra bound it with weirding to the rocks below, welding them one to another so they formed a single, solid whole. And when the final piece was placed, she returned the overspill to its normal course, and the water began to gather behind the stone blockade.

Yet the feed of water was slight; it would take many months to fill the apportioned ravine. In the meantime, the bed of the stream lay dry below, a pebbled snake now grey and dead.

When the Skgaro noticed her labors, they questioned her. Ilgra merely claimed that she wanted to make a larger pool for swimming, and the clan did not see fit to challenge her word, ascribing her actions to the expected eccentricities of a shaman.

But while her explanation satisfied the rest of the clan, it did not satisfy her mother, who said, "You never do anything without purpose, Ilgra-daughter. Tell me truly, what is it you want?"

Then it was Ilgra's loneliness proved her undoing. A moment of weakness overcame her—a desire for much-missed closeness with those she loved—and in that moment of weakness, she confessed her secret desire.

The confession greatly angered her mother, and she said, "*This* is why you have kept yourself apart, Ilgra-daughter? It is head-sickness. It is dog-bite fever. The dragon cannot be killed. If ever he leaves, it will be of his own choice, and not because of anything we have done."

To which Ilgra said, "That I cannot accept. I will either kill Vêrmund, or he will kill me. No other outcome is possible."

Her mother gnashed her teeth. "Why must you be so troublesome? Some things there are we cannot change. There is no glory in fighting the inevitable. Do you not understand?"

"I understand that the worm killed my father, who was your bloodmate! You would leave him and the rest of our clanmates unavenged. Well not I!"

Then Ilgra's mother locked horns with her, though the difference in their height was so great as to make Ilgra bend nearly in half. "I honored my mate, and I cared for our children," said her mother, a growl in her voice. "There was no glory in getting myself slain that you might grow up alone in the world."

At that, understanding broke Ilgra's anger, and she bared her throat. "You are right. I meant no disrespect."

Her mother lifted her horns as well. A softness entered her expression. "You are a good daughter to me, Ilgra, and a good sister to Yhana. But please, give up this fruitless quest. It will bring you nothing but sorrow."

"I cannot."

"You are determined? You will spend your life in this manner, despite my counsel?"

"I am."

And her mother sighed. "Then I must give

you my blessing in the hope it may prove a shield against misfortune." And she did so, and they em-braced, and Ilgra felt her eyes fill with tears.

Early next morning, Ilgra came out of her hut to find Yhana standing upon the side of the ra-vine, staring at Ilgra's handiwork below.

Said her sister, "You still mean to avenge our father." It was not a question.

To which Ilgra said, "Yes."

Then Yhana looked at her with fierce eyes. "Good. Were I as strong as you, I would do likewise. You are Anointed, but I am not. You know the ways of weirding, but I do not. And you have no fear, Ilgra-sister. I wish the same were true for me."

"I do fear," said Ilgra. "But it does not stop me." Then she wrapped Yhana in her arms, and it com-forted Ilgra to know her sister supported her and shared her desire to stop Vêrmund.

Her family said nothing to the rest of the Skgaro of Ilgra's intent, and for that Ilgra was grateful. But thereafter, she felt more alone than ever, for the weight of Yhana's expectations added to her own, and the voice of the wind seemed to acquire a mocking tone.

While she waited for the ravine to fill, she focused her energies on her duties as shaman to the Skgaro. Mainly this involved helping with births, healing what hurts she could, and setting spells upon various tools as a guard against breakage or other mishap. A shaman's responsibilities were of a more tangible sort than those of the Herndall—who, along with leading the clan, oversaw the mysteries of auguries and portents, as well as all matters pertaining to the gods. It was for the best. Despite her use of weirding, Ilgra preferred to deal with things that she could touch. Things that were real.

The Horned she assisted often gave her gifts in return; the saving of a life was no small thing, after all. By such means, Ilgra soon acquired a small herd of sheep and goats (and one disgruntled bristle-back boar). She penned the animals within the ravine and fed them each day with fodder kept dry beneath a stand of layered branches. Also, about the pen she hung woven charms, so as to fend off the beasts of the mountains.

Thus it was she baited her trap.

The filling of the ravine went far slower than Ilgra expected. It worried her, for winter was nigh, and at least once each winter, Vêrmund would descend for a smallish meal of whatever livestock he could catch. If the gorge was only partially full by the time he came to eat, the wash of water would be insufficient to subdue the mighty worm, and she would have to wait through the winter, until the worm's next feeding.

Faced with that unpleasant prospect, Ilgra decided to take drastic measures. She went to the spring-fed pool above the ravine and, by the strength of her limbs, dug a channel through the full height of the bank, that the pool might drain unhindered into the ravine below. The water was less than she needed, but with its addition, she had hope the reservoir might fill in time.

If Vêrmund the Grim noticed her work, Ilgra knew he would never be so foolish as to enter the ravine. He was a canny old worm and wary of ambush. Fortunately, the steep-sided flanks of Kulkaras hid the pool from the dragon's burning eyes, and Ilgra felt confident of catching him un- awares.

Otherwise, her plans would end in fire.

▽ ▽ ▽

Three moons passed before the stream finally filled the dam, tumbled over the cracked and weathered lip, and continued along its ancestral bed. Winter had settled upon the valley during the third moon, and shingles of broken ice covered the newly formed pool, now dark with shadowed depths. The ice pleased Ilgra; it made the trap that much more dangerous. To further increase the damage the water might cause upon release, she rolled windfell trees atop the ice, until a thicket of brittle branches adorned the frozen pool.

Thereafter, all that was left was to wait for Vêrmund to bestir himself. It would not be long, she thought, before hunger woke the worm from his evil sleep.

In those days, Ilgra kept to her hut, insisting that the Skgaro come to her whenever possible, lest she find herself too far afield when Vêrmund finally came thundering down. It was a selfish insistence, and her mother disapproved, but her clanmates never complained, again accepting Ilgra's demand as normal of a shaman. For that, she felt ashamed. But shame could not sway her from her course.

Long hours she spent in isolation, sitting and brooding while she turned her mind to the twisting of words. With each night that passed, she felt more withdrawn, as if she were fading from the world, becoming a wraith haunting the dark pinewood forest.

She thought much of her father during those days. Of how in winter he sat by the hearth and wove the *thulqna*, the patterned straps by which the Horned display the crest of their clan and also the lineage of their families, with all the notable deeds ascribed to their ancestors. Of how he carved figures of deer and goats and foxes for her and Yhana to play with. Of how safe she had felt beside him, so large and strong was he.

Then too Ilgra recalled an evening when she was hardly more than a babe, and her father had returned from the hunt with a doe draped over his shoulder. The eyes of the deer had been so round and soft they had troubled Ilgra, and she had been greatly saddened by the sight. But her father knelt beside her, and he said, "Do not be upset, Ilgra-daughter. There is nothing to fear. This is the way of things. Today we feed upon the deer that we may live. In time, our bodies will feed the grass and trees that other deer may live. So it goes."

Ilgra had once found the thought comforting. No more, though. Her mind rebelled against the truth of what her father said, insisted that there must be another, better way.

Just because something *was* did not mean it should always be.

The winter solstice marked a break in her self-imposed exile. It was a time of celebration for the Skgaro as they said a welcome farewell to the shortest day of the year. In the village there was much music and feasting to be had and feats of strength also, cheered on by the whole of the clan.

Ilgra waited out the first part of the festivities in her hut, waited until the light began to fade from the sky and she felt certain Vêrmund was not about to fly down. Never yet had he attacked during night, and she doubted his habit was about to change. Regardless, leaving her post by the ravine was worth the risk. She felt in sore need of company; the sounds of song drifting from the village put a pang in her heart.

A layer of heavy clouds hung over the valley, and from them fell soft flakes of snow, large and slow. In the muffled solitude, Ilgra trudged from her hut to the village and thence to her family hall. Along the way, she heard the baying of hungry wolves echoing through the forest. Had she not her staff, Ilgra would have feared for her life.

She spent the evening with her mother and Yhana, cooking and talking and enjoying the pleasure of their closeness. Later still, they played games and lamented the length of winter, while outside the flurries of snow thickened into a blinding wall, driven before the relentless, ice-cut wind.

Then a shriek pierced the storm-wrapped night, a shriek such as Ilgra had never heard before. At the sound of it, her heart clenched and her bones grew cold and every bristle on her nape prickled and stood on end. For a moment, she could neither move nor breathe, and only when her heart finally jolted back to life was she able to properly react.

"What *was* that?" whispered her mother.

And Ilgra knew not. Nothing in Qarzhad's teaching had spoken of such a thing. Another shriek, louder than before, split the wind, and Ilgra shivered from head to toe. She grabbed Gorgoth and sprang to her feet.

Before she could take a step, a great black beak stabbed through the roof and struck the hearth fire, spraying sparks and coals in every direction. Again and again the beak struck, snapping and swiping, while a purple tongue lashed with frenzied anger between the two halves.

Ilgra shouted and smote the beak upon the side and spoke a word of weirding: *garjzla*, or *light*.

A ruddy flash blinded her, and with a deafening screech, the beak withdrew. Then the hall shuddered, and two sets of huge, hooked claws began to rip at the roof, pulling the timbered beams apart. Blasts of swirling snow poured in through the rents.

"Run!" shouted Ilgra to her mother and sister, and together they fled the hall.

Outside, in the cold and the dark, Ilgra heard more shrieks, and as her blood curdled in her veins, she saw squatting atop the peak of their hall a firelit monstrosity. The creature was grey and hairless and lean as a starveling. Bat wings hung from its shoulders, and at the end of its ropy neck was a gaunt and narrow skull set with a pair of enormous black eyes—bulging and devoid of white—and then the long dagger of its beak. Across the village, tattered sheets of snow parted to reveal a second monster prowling between the buildings, pecking at the Horned as they ran, crimson streaks of gore banding its beak.

The creatures reminded Ilgra not of any beast of earth or sky, but rather of beings from ancient legend: the loathsome Nrech. Killers of Svarvok's infant sons. Eaters of Horned. Foul shadows that stalked the land of the dead, picking clean the bones of dishonored warriors.

Terror poisoned her thoughts.

As if in response, the near creature turned its head and darted snake-like toward Ilgra and her family. They ran, and for a brief while, the storm hid them. Ilgra heard Arvog and Moqtar and Razhag and the rest of the warriors shouting as they strove to fight the Nrech. Through gaps in the snow, she glimpsed the defenders gathered by torchlight, holding spears pointed toward the oncoming monstrosities. But the creatures were too big and too fast; they towered over even the Anointed, and their beaks were like those of cranes—quick and deadly as they jabbed through the clotted air.

Ilgra raised her staff then and set forth to work what magic she could. But her weirding had no power over the Nrech; they were somehow shielded against her words, and all her attacks went awry. Nor could she blind or bind or otherwise slow them.

Ahead of her, she saw Elgha speared by one of the Nrech, speared and eaten, the starveling consuming the Herndall with two gulping motions.

Razhag ran forth and was knocked aside, with bloody wounds torn across his arms.

The familiar heaviness of despair weighed upon Ilgra's heart. There was no stopping the Nrech. She looked to Kulkaras, hidden within the baffling smear of the blizzard, and for the first and only time, Ilgra wished for the help of Vêrmund the Grim. And she wondered *why* the miserable old worm hadn't risen in protest, as he had once before.

The wind grew stronger until it moaned with dire voice through her horns, and Ilgra realized; the storm had dampened the sounds of the attack, hid the clamor of fear and death within its folds. The dragon could not have heard upon his lofty perch.

Ilgra knew then what must be done, though the thought replaced her despair with shriveling fear.

With both her hands, she planted Gorgoth upright in the snow, and she spoke a word of weirding to the wind, and for a span, the air grew clear and still. Then, from her knotted belt, Ilgra took her father's horn, and she sounded it with all her hope and might, and the brazen call rang forth throughout the valley.

Twice more Ilgra blew upon the horn. Then one of the Nrech came crawling toward her, and she allowed the snow to close in around her once again.

Yet still no response returned from the crown of Kulkaras. No hint of Vêrmund stirring. No hope of calamitous rescue. This time the dragon's indifference would be the death of them.

Believing her gambit had failed, Ilgra found her family and started with them toward a burrow where they might hide.

And then . . . she heard the sound of their destroyer, and for once she was glad. She heard the rumble of Vêrmund's wrath, and the air convulsed with a jarring thud, and a blast of wind from the dragon's wings swept aside the falling snow in whorls and pennants and twisting braids.

In the darkness cleared, the Nrech crouched, shrieking with eager hate. They leaped to flight and climbed with startling speed toward the bulky, firelit mass of Vêrmund descending from above.

"Go," Ilgra said, pushing her mother and sister toward the burrow. But she herself stayed; not even the threat of death could tear her away.

Vêrmund roared and seared the night sky with flames. Quick as sparrows, the Nrech swooped away and flew around either side of the dragon and began to peck and claw at his back. The worm bellowed in pain, tucked in his wings, and dove to ground in a meadow near the village. The creatures followed, harrying him closely, nipping and biting and tearing at his wings.

Ilgra rose from hiding and started to run

toward her hut by the dam. The villagers had fled their halls, and from the cover of the forest, Arvog hailed her, motioned for her to join him.

Instead, she lowered her head as if to ram her foes and increased her speed.

Behind her, Vêrmund continued to bellow with pain and anger, cries Ilgra had long wished to hear of him but that now only filled her with dread. She glanced from the dark path before her, checking the positions of the nightmares fighting.

The Nrech were faster than the old worm, and they seemed accustomed to contending with dragons, for they knew when to dodge his fire and how also to avoid his teeth, talons, and tail. Vêrmund snapped and snarled as he tried to lure them within range of his deadly claws, but the grey creatures were too smart and stayed at a safe distance, moving in only when the dragon's back was turned.

The three giants battled across the fields,

and the mountains rang with the clamor, a horrendous sound. Gouts of liquid flame sprayed the landscape, and along the edges of the forest, the tips of branches caught fire—makeshift torches bright enough to illuminate the whole of the valley, though they sputtered beneath their load of snow.

Vêrmund slammed his tail into the ground, and so great was the impact, it shook Ilgra off her feet, sent her tumbling forward onto her face. The crusted snow cut her brow, and she grunted as the air rushed from her lungs. Hot blood poured over her eyes, blinding her. She shook her head, sprang back up, and continued running.

The Nrech were ripping bleeding chunks from Vêrmund's scaled length; his natural armor provided little protection against their beaks. His roars acquired a desperate edge, a wounded bull faced with a pair of red-toothed mountain cats, savage and merciless.

And still Ilgra ran. Her once-broken leg lacked strength. Her breath burned in her throat. She could barely see the path rising before her and, beside it, the dark crevice of the ravine.

A blob of fluttering fire arced past, and she ducked out of instinct. The fire splashed against a nearby rock, a welcome light upon the glittering snow.

Below, in the depths of the gorge, her small flock yammered with terror. She heard the pen give way before their panicked efforts, and then the animals fled the confines of the ravine, bleating all the while. She did not mind. Bait they had been, but now they might perhaps survive.

At last Ilgra's destination came in sight: the dam, mantled with cobwebs of silver frost. With loping steps, Ilgra climbed the bank and stopped upon the shore of ice-capped water.

She stood, panting and coughing, blood streaming from her brow—stood and looked back at the

mangled earth where Vêrmund and the Nrech
still contended in mortal combat. The beasts had
pressed Vêrmund back against the edge of the
trees, where the rise of the land toward the mountains limited his movement. Even as Ilgra watched,
one of the creatures pounced on the dragon's left
wing, bearing it to the ground, while the other
clawed its way across his ribs until it reached the
base of his neck.

Vêrmund writhed in a frantic attempt to shake
off his attackers, but the monstrosities kept a firm
hold on him. The one clinging to his neck pecked,
and the evil old worm coiled in upon himself, hiding his head under his body.

The Nrech shrieked with triumph as they
closed in on the dragon's exposed side, their wings
held high.

"No!" said Ilgra, afraid she'd missed her chance.
She could break the dam, but the creatures were
too far away to be assured of their deaths (and

Vêrmund's as well). Somehow she had to draw them closer, where the wall of water could do its work.

Desperate, Ilgra reached for Vêrmund with her mind. She found him, but she could not make him understand; the dragon was too addled by pain to notice her feeble thoughts. In comparison to his consciousness, Ilgra was a nothing, a guttering fleck of light beside the raging conflagration that was the dragon's inner being.

With a start, Ilgra returned to herself. Convulsions of panic seized her heart. Time was short; if she did not act *now*, all would be lost. They might finally be rid of Vêrmund, but in his place they would be left with the Nrech, and the Nrech had not the restraint of the dragon. They would kill every one of the Skgaro and make a nest of their bones upon the crest of Kulkaras. This she knew from the stories.

On the claw-torn fields, Vêrmund thrashed beneath the pecking monstrosities.

Then an idea dawned bright and fierce upon Ilgra. The horn had roused the old worm from his sleep and summoned him to the fight. If he heard it again, perhaps he would understand, perhaps . . .

She took a half step forward, lifted her father's horn, placed it against her lips, and blew forth with such strength that the echoes chased themselves from one end of the valley to the other. Beyond the village, she saw her clanmates emerge from the fringe of flickering shadow and look toward her hut, frightened, curious, wondering— she felt sure—if her call were a summons.

It was, but not for them. Ilgra waved at them to keep back, though she doubted they could see. She hoped they would stay well clear of the ravine, lest they be killed or swept away.

She was about to sound the horn a second time when Vêrmund uttered a crackling roar and heaved upward, tossing the flapping monstrosities to either side. Battered and wounded though he was, with blood streaming from scores of wounds, the dragon was still stronger by far than either of the Nrech.

He staggered forward, each crashing step causing Ilgra to lose her balance and snow to fall in sifting veils from the silent trees. The Nrech shrieked as one and bounded after, throwing themselves at Vêrmund's neck and shoulders. The dragon snarled and leaped toward the mouth of the ravine, half opening his tattered wings so his leap became a long glide.

As Vêrmund landed amid the icy drifts within the narrow gorge, he sent a spray of glittering crystals singing upward.

And Ilgra knew her moment had arrived.

She took her staff then, and with it smote the

top of the dam. In a voice terrible to hear, she uttered a single weirding word: *jierda—break!* The
word was a key with which she unlocked the tem-
pest of power trapped within Gorgoth and sent
the whole whirling confusion into the stones
of the dam.

The dam cracked and shuddered, and the bank
Ilgra stood upon sagged alarmingly. She scrambled
back to more solid footing.

Granite split with explosive force, and ice too,
as the surface of the pool broke asunder, shoot-
ing frozen shards in every direction. Then, with
a rumble louder than Vêrmund's deepest roars,
the dam gave way, and a wall of water, ice, and
windfell trees raced down the ravine and slammed
into Vêrmund and the Nrech. The churning torrent washed over the three, enveloping them in a
surge of foam, and Ilgra heard the creak and pop
of colliding ice and the groan of twisting timber.

Beneath the water, huge shapes turned and

thrashed before falling still. The spikes along Vêrmund's back soon breached the surface—he was
too large to stay submerged for long—but they
remained where they were, motionless: a stationary sieve that logs and branches fetched up against
until his back was a mound of jagged wood.

Ilgra clung to the ground as it rolled beneath
her, and she prayed to Rahna and Svarvok and all
the other gods besides.

The water was swift to subside, draining away
through the fields to the south, carrying with it a
pair of bleating goats. Then Ilgra braced herself
on Gorgoth and slowly got to her feet.

She beheld her handiwork. There, in a
crumpled heap in the now-empty ravine, lay the
mighty Vêrmund, and with him the two monstrosities: one beneath the worm's serrated claws,
its neck crooked at an unnatural angle, and one
deposited some distance to the east in a tangle of
grey-skinned limbs.

The vast bellows of Vêrmund's ribs still moved, but feebly, and the wrinkled old worm otherwise displayed no sign of life. No hint of smoke trailed from his nostrils. No glow of fire emanated from between his gaping jaws. And no sign of movement appeared between his slitted lids.

▽   ▽   ▽

A rising, bursting feel of triumph swelled Ilgra's breast. Now was her chance! If she struck quick and true, she might finally rid the world of Vêrmund's blight and finally be avenged of her father's death. She would carve out the worm's blackened heart, and when it was hers, burn it before the gods as thanks for their favor.

She hurried down the path along the ravine, moving as fast as her leg would allow. The dragon's breathing was already growing louder; she had only a brief while in which to act.

Just as she reached the base of the hill, a voice rang out:

"Ilgra!"

Her sister ran toward Vêrmund from the edge of the forest, a knife held high in one hand, teeth bared in a battle face.

"Back!" Ilgra shouted, but Yhana listened not. She seemed intent on cutting the throat of the dragon herself, and it struck Ilgra then—for the first time—that her sister was no longer a youngling. She was full-grown and as willing to fight as any of the Skgaro.

A clutch of conflicting emotions warred within Ilgra. Selfishness and concern and surprise. Then she decided, and with her decision came a sense of solidarity; they could kill the dragon together.

Before she could call out to Yhana again, Ilgra was horrified to see the far Nrech stir. Rising on broken limbs, it swung its head back and forth, blindly scenting for prey. A jagged shriek tore free of the creature's throat, and it began to scrabble after Yhana, dragging its useless wings across the frozen mess of the field.

At the sound, a shudder ran the length of Vêrmund's body. And Ilgra knew, if she helped Yhana, she would lose all chance of killing the dragon. He would regain his feet, and even wounded and weakened, he still far outmatched them. Ilgra no longer had the great storehouse of energy in Gorgoth to rely upon, only that of her body, and the strength of her body paled in comparison with that of the dragon's.

The strain of anguish rent Ilgra's heart, but in the end, there was only one choice. Howling with fear and fury, she charged past the fallen dragon and to her sister's side.

As the snapping Nrech fell upon them, Ilgra raised Gorgoth, drew upon the reserves of power within her flesh, and shouted, *"Brisingr!"* A fountain of fire erupted from the end of the staff and bathed the monstrosity's head with a torrent of flame.

The Nrech recoiled and shrieked again, so loud that Ilgra lost her will and the fire faded to dark. In that instant, she knew with certainty she was about to die, eaten by a nightmare from ages past. And her sister too, slain by the failure of Ilgra's ambitions.

Then the clacking beak of the Nrech stabbed toward them and the earth shook with sudden violence. A streak of black scales appeared overhead, a foul wind swept the field, and a great *crack* sounded, frightening in its deathly finality.

Ilgra cowered, covering her sister with her arms. When she dared look again, she saw the black bulk of Vêrmund standing over them, stark against the swirling snow. And hanging between the worm's enormous jaws, the now-limp monstrosity, its body pierced through and through by rows of glistening teeth.

The godkillers were slain.

For a moment, Ilgra felt relief. Gratitude, even. But both reactions paled before a sickening sense of doom. She had been so close to her desire. So close, and yet once again it had slipped her grasp. And now she and Yhana were caught beneath the devouring dragon.

Vêrmund snuffed and let fall the grey corpse, obscene in its hairless shape. Then he shook his head as a dog might, and drops of steaming blood rained upon the flood-swept land. One bead, dark and gleaming, splattered across Ilgra's arm, and she cried out as it burned her skin, hot as molten lead.

Vêrmund took notice. He looked down and then lowered his head until the blazing void of his eye hung before them, terrifying in its nearness.

Ilgra stifled the urge to flee, for they could not hope to outrun the dragon. Nor could they hope to best it with blades or weirding. Defiant to the end, she stood her tallest while Yhana clung to her arm.

Then Ilgra felt the dragon's mind upon her own, huge and bleak and daunting. From it came no thanks, no approval, no care or consideration. But there was one thought, one impression, Ilgra received from the worm:

Recognition. No longer was Vêrmund indifferent. He acknowledged her existence, and from him came a sense of interest, detached and impersonal though it was. He might still view her as prey, but by her actions, Ilgra had earned a measure of regard from the battered old worm.

It was no small thing.

Seven heartbeats they remained as thus, locked in close embrace. Seven heartbeats only, and then the towering immensity of his mind withdrew, and Vêrmund snorted and his hot breath washed over Ilgra in a choking wave of sulfurous scent.

Her vision grew blurred, and Ilgra dropped to one knee, faint. Then Vêrmund stepped over them, the pallid scales of his belly rimmed with twinkling fire from the forest, and the chill of his shadow lifted from their shoulders.

Ilgra screwed shut her eyes and stayed where she had fallen, stayed until the ground grew still and the sound of Vêrmund's tread had faded to a distant toll.

It was the touch of her sister's hand that roused her. "Ilgra! He is gone! We are saved."

Only then did she stand and look.

The worm had a wounded wing; he could not fly. Instead, he crawled up the face of bold Kulkaras with slow and weary steps, leaving behind a trail of blood and broken trees. He seemed like to fall, never to rise again, and Ilgra wondered if they might yet be freed of him.

She had to know.

Ere long, the sheets of snow obscured the dragon. Yhana tugged on Ilgra's tunic, urged her to leave, said, "You have done all you can. Our father's death is not avenged, but we have honored his memory. There is no more. Come now." But Ilgra refused, preferring to stand and watch and listen to Vêrmund's painful progress.

The order of things was not yet settled.

Farther up the valley, the rest of the Skgaro began to emerge from hiding. Arvog and several of the other warriors trotted out with weapons in hand, joined Ilgra and Yhana there on that muddy tract.

They checked the Nrech to ensure the monstrosities would bedevil their clan never again. Then they spoke to Ilgra, thanked her, praised her, cajoled her, berated her. But regardless, she would not move.

At last they left her, Yhana as well—left her that they might tend their injured and save their belongings from what halls were damaged.

And there Ilgra stayed, until she heard the distant sound of talons scraping against stone, and then from the peak of Kulkaras, Vêrmund the Grim let loose a mighty roar, and he painted the clouds with fire such that brightened the whole of the night.

Then he grew still and silent, and Ilgra knew: the dragon would not die, and they, poor sufferers, would not be rid of him.

Ilgra grasped her staff with both hands and leaned upon it. Her heart was too small to contain all her feeling; she shouted after Vêrmund, though the dragon would not hear, and every part of her was wracked with turmoil.

Ragged gaps appeared in the snow as the storm began to clear, and through them she saw the crown of Kulkaras, and perched thereon, the looming shape of Vêrmund the Grim.

Ilgra stared at him for a silent while. Then she breathed deep of the freezing air and, with her exhale, released her torment. So. One thing had become clear: there would always be a stalking hunger waiting to eat them. If not Vêrmund, then the monstrosities. If not the monstrosities, then some other, equally horrible creature. It was a basic fact of life, as true for the Horned as it was for every other being. None were exempt: not bear nor wolf nor cat nor even the most fearsome of hunters. All fell prey in time. It was not a question of *if* but *when*.

Vêrmund had saved them from the monstrosities. Without him, the Nrech might have slain the entire village. Yet Ilgra knew they could expect no great mercy from him thereafter. It was not in his nature. He would continue to fly down upon them and eat their herds and trample their fields and slaughter those foolish enough to attack him. So it was and always would be.

Someday Ilgra would again face the dragon. Someday he would come ravening toward her, or else she would once more climb Kulkaras and go to meet him in single combat. It was a certainty. Whenever they met, whether next year or long after her hair turned grey, Ilgra felt sure of one thing: that Vêrmund would know her and remember her, and though he would give her no quarter, she would at least have the satisfaction of his recognition.

But for now, her quest was at an end. The dam was broken and the pool of water drained. Likewise Gorgoth. And though Vêrmund was sore wounded, Ilgra no longer had the means or inclination to confront him. Not then. Nor did she believe it would do any good. Hurt or not, the dragon was more than a match for her, for the

Skgaro, and even for creatures born of darkest legend, as were the Nrech.

A figure came walking from the village: her mother, bearing a blanket and salve for wounds. She wrapped the blanket around Ilgra's shoulders and applied the salve to her arm, where Vêrmund's blood had burned her raw.

Said her mother, "Come now, Ilgra-daughter, leave this unhappy place. Return with me to where you belong."

And Ilgra felt as if woken from a dream.

She turned her back, then—turned her back on the worm resting in his bloody slumber; turned her back on tall, snow-mantled Kulkaras; turned her back on the remnants of the dam and on her hut besides. She turned her back on all those things and, with her mother, started the slow walk to the village, leaning upon her staff with every step.

No longer would she stand apart. That time had passed. Once again she would join in the clan's

daily life. She would claim a mate, she thought—
Arvog, perhaps—and bear his children. In all manner possible, she would drink to the dregs each day
and worry not what fate might bring.

Ilgra looked at the staff. It was Gorgoth no
more, she decided, but rather Warung, or *Acceptance*.
And the now-empty sapphire a legacy in waiting, a
potential that she might, with time and effort, re-
store to its former glory.

She straightened her back and bared her teeth,
feeling given new purpose. For her name was Ilgra
Nrech-Slayer, and she feared no evil.

✦   ✦   ✦

CHAPTER IX

New Beginnings

The last words of Irsk's telling faded to silence in the main hall of the hold, high on Mount Arn-gor. Then the Urgal struck the drum between his knees, and a dull, booming note reverberated off the stone walls, marking an end to the story.

Eragon blinked and rubbed his face, feeling as if he too were waking from a dream. Around the hearth, the rest of the Urgals likewise stirred, stat-ues coming to life.

With a growl, Skarghaz shoved himself to his feet and strode over to where Irsk sat. He grabbed the smaller Urgal by the horns and, with a violent, jerking motion, butted him in the head.

The Urgals roared with laughter, and Skarghaz said, "Well done, Irsk! Well said. You do your clan proud."

The impact knocked Irsk back, but he bared his teeth in a fierce grin and—with just as much vigor—butted Skarghaz in return. "Honor for the clan, Nar Skarghaz."

The fire had burned down to a bed of coals, and a chill had crept into the air while Irsk told his tale. Eragon glanced out the windows, wondering at the hour. The sky was black, without so much as a glimmer of the silver moon, and even the round-eyed owls that roosted in the dark pine trees were silent in their nests. It was late—far later than he made a habit of staying up—but he didn't mind.

"That was a most excellent story, Irsk," he said, and bowed as best he could while sitting. "Thank you." He understood now why the Kull had requested that particular story, and Eragon was glad of it. It seemed there was always something for him to learn, even from the Urgals.

What did you think? he asked Saphira.

Approval radiated from her. *I liked Ilgra. And I liked Vêrmund even more. It is only right that the dragon would win.*

Eragon smiled slightly. Then he said out loud, "Was that a true story?"

"Of course it was a true story!" exclaimed Skarghaz, stomping back to his chair. "We would not tell you a story that said wrong things about the world, Rider."

"No, I mean, did it really happen? Did Ilgra actually exist? And Vêrmund, and the mountain Kulkaras?"

Skarghaz scratched his chin, a thoughtful look in his yellow eyes. "It is an old story, Rider. Perhaps going back to the time before our kind crossed the sea. But I think the story happened as it says. . . .

Even to this day, the Urgralgra often name their daughters Ilgra, and because of her, every one of us knows that there is a Vêrmund we cannot best. It is a good lesson to learn, I think."

"A good lesson indeed," said Eragon. In some ways, he had defeated his own Vêrmund in the person of Galbatorix, but there were still things in life he could not overcome—things that no one could. It was a sobering thought. When Eragon was younger, the knowledge would have bothered him to no end. Now, though, he understood the wisdom of acceptance. Even if it didn't make him happy, it at least gave him peace, and that was no small gift.

Happiness, Eragon had decided, was a fleeting, futile thing to pursue. Contentment, on the other hand, was a far more worthwhile goal.

"The Anointed," he said, "are those—"

"What in our tongue we call the Kull," said Irsk.

Eragon had thought as much. "And the Nrech,

they are Lethrblaka?" A shadow seemed to descend upon the hall as he named the creatures.

Skarghaz coughed. "Gah! Yes, if you must speak of the blasted things, yes. We are fortunate you killed the last of them, Rider. And you as well, dragon." He nodded toward Saphira, who blinked once in return.

"If we are so lucky," said Eragon under his breath. Many a night he still wondered about Galbatorix's claim to have hidden more of the Ra'zac's eggs throughout Alagaësia. For Ra'zac, once grown, transformed into Lethrblaka, as caterpillars into butterflies. Even with all Eragon knew of magic, the thought of having to again face the creatures, Ra'zac or Lethrblaka both, was unsettling indeed.

A commotion sounded at the back of the hall, and at the same time, he sensed a disturbance among the Eldunarí in the Hall of Colors.

Alarmed, he struggled to his feet. Saphira hissed and did the same, her claws scrabbling on the floor.

Blödhgarm, Ästrith, Rílven, and the rest of
the elves hurried toward them from across the
hall. The elves were smiling—beautiful, broad,
white-toothed smiles—and their steps were quick
and light. It was such a contrast with their usual
decorum, Eragon wasn't sure how to react. He
would have found scowls and blank, impassive
expressions far less unnerving.

"Ebrithil," said Blödhgarm, the midnight-blue
fur along his shoulders rippling with excitement.

"What's wrong?" said Eragon. Behind him, he
heard stomps and clatters as the Urgals gathered
in ranks, as if they expected the elves to attack.
At the same time, the minds of the Eldunarí were
a riot of conflicting words, thoughts, images, and
emotions—a storm of sensations that made Eragon
wince and that defied his attempts to decipher.

Saphira shook herself and growled, baring her
long white fangs.

Blödhgarm's smile widened, and he laughed in

a delighted fashion. "Nothing is wrong, Ebrithil. Quite the opposite, in fact; everything is right with the world."

Then Ästrith said, "One of the eggs has hatched."

Eragon blinked. "One of—"

"A dragon has hatched, Ebrithil!" said Blödh-garm. "Another dragon is born!"

Saphira craned back her neck and crowed toward the shadowed ceiling, and the Urgals stomped and shouted until the entire hall rang with the sounds of celebration.

Eragon grinned, and he threw his cup over his head and let loose with an entirely undignified whoop. All of their hard work—all of the late nights and early mornings, the spells that left him exhausted and the endless worrying about provisions and politics and people—all of it had been worth it.

A new beginning had dawned for the dragons.

Names and Languages

On the Origin of Names:

To the casual observer, the various names an intrepid traveler will encounter throughout Alagaësia might seem but a random collection with no inherent integrity, culture, or history. However, as with any land that different groups—and in this case, different species—have repeatedly colonized, Alagaësia acquired names from a wide array of unique sources, among them the languages of the dwarves, elves, humans, and even Urgals. Thus we can have Palancar Valley (a human name), the Anora River and Ristvak'baen (elven names), and Utgard Mountain (a dwarven name) all within a few square miles of each other.

While this is of great historical interest, practically it often leads to confusion as to the correct pronunciation. Unfortunately, there are no set rules for the neophyte. You must learn each name upon its own terms, unless you can immediately place its language of origin. The matter grows even more confusing when you realize that in many places the resident population altered the spelling and pronunciation of foreign words to conform to their own language. The Anora River is a prime example. Originally *anora* was spelled *äenora*, which means *broad* in the ancient language. In their writings, the humans simplified the word to *anora*, and this, combined with a vowel shift wherein *äe* (ay-eh) was said as the easier *a* (uh), created the name as it appears in Eragon's time.

To spare readers as much difficulty as possible, I

have compiled the following list, with the understanding that these are only rough guidelines to
the actual pronunciation. The enthusiast is encouraged to study the source languages in order to
master their true intricacies.

PRONUNCIATION:

Alagaësia—al-uh-GAY-zee-uh

Arya—AR-ee-uh

Ästrith—AY-strith

Blödhgarm—BLAWD-garm

Brisingr—BRISS-ing-gur

Du Weldenvarden—doo WELL-den-VAR-den

Ellesméra—el-uhs-MEER-uh

Eragon—EHR-uh-gahn

Galbatorix—gal-buh-TOR-icks

Gil'ead—GILL-ee-id

Glaedr—GLAY-dur

Hruthmund—HRUTH-mund

Ilgra—ILL-gruh

Irsk—URSK

Kulkaras—kull-CAR-us

Murtagh—MUR-tag (*mur* rhymes with *purr*)

Nasuada—nah-soo-AH-dah

Oromis—OR-uh-miss

Qarzhad—KWAR-zhahd

Ra'zac—RAA-zack

Rílven—REAL-ven (*ríl* is a hard sound to transcribe; it's made by flicking the tip of the tongue off the roof of the mouth)

Saphira—suh-FEAR-uh

Skarghaz—SCAR-ghawzh

Tronjheim—TRONJ-heem

Ulkrö—ULL-kroh

Umaroth—oo-MAR-oth

Urû'baen—OO-roo-bane

Vêrmund—VAIR-mooned

Yhana—YHAW-nuh

THE ANCIENT LANGUAGE:

Argetlam—Silver Hand

Atra esterní ono thelduin.—May good fortune rule over you.

Blödhgarm—Bloodwolf

brisingr—fire

du—the

Du Vrangr Gata—The Wandering Path

Du Weldenvarden—The Guarding Forest

Ebrithil—Master

Eldunarí—a dragon's heart of hearts

Fell Thindarë—Mountain of Night

finiarel—male honorific for a young one of great
   promise

garjzla—light

jierda—break; hit

Kvetha Fricaya—Greetings, Friends

Lethrblaka—Leather-Flapper

melthna—melt

rïsa—rise

Shur'tugal—Dragon Rider

vaeta—hope

DWARVISH:

Arngor—White Mountain

barzûl—to curse someone with ill fate

beor—cave bear (borrowed from the ancient language)

dûrgrimst—clan (literally, "our hall" or "our home")

gor—mountain

Gor Narrveln—Mountain of Gems

Ingeitum—fire workers; smiths

Jurgencarmeitder—Dragon Rider

Mûnnvlorss—a type of dwarven mead

Tronjheim—Helm of Giants

URGALISH:

drajl—spawn of maggots

gorgoth—revenge

Herndall—a group of elderly dams who rule
an Urgal clan; also an individual dam who
belongs to said group

Maghra—an Urgal game of chance and strategy

nar—a title of great respect

Nrech—Lethrblaka

ozhthim—a female Urgal's first monthly blood

rekk—an Urgal drink made from fermented
cattails

thulqna—woven strips Urgals use to display the
crests of their clans, as well as the deeds and
lineage of their families

Ungvek—Strong-Headed

Urgralgra—the Urgals' name for themselves
(literally, "those with horns")

warung—acceptance

AFTERWORD

FROM CHRISTOPHER:

Kvetha Fricaya. Greetings, Friends.

It's been a while. . . .

This was an unplanned-for book. A bit over two years ago, I wrote the first version of "The Worm of Kulkaras" as a means of clearing my head between sections of a larger sci-fi project. Although I was pleased with it, "Worm" by itself was too short to publish. Thus it sat on my computer, alone and abandoned, until the summer of 2018.

At that point, I got an urge to write a story about Murtagh I'd long had in mind. This became "A Fork in the Road." I sent both that and "Worm" off to my editor at Knopf. Meanwhile, my sister, Angela, proposed writing a vignette from her character's point of view. And hey, presto! Before I knew it, we were in talks to release this anthology that same year. (For those of you not familiar with publishing, that is a highly accelerated schedule.)

I'd always imagined returning to Alagaësia with a full-sized novel. However, doing it this way made for a wonderful experience. Getting to dip into the heads of some of the characters from the Inheritance Cycle—as well as a few new ones— was a real treat for me. Writing about Eragon and Saphira after so many years was like returning home after a long journey.

Plus, I finally proved to myself that I could turn out a book that was shorter than 500 pages. Success!

Short it may be, but as with every book, *The Fork, the Witch, and the Worm* would not exist without the hard work of a whole team of people:

My wonderful parents, who continue to provide the same love, support, and editing as they have all my life. I owe them more than I can say. Couldn't have done this without you!

My sister, Angela, who still has a good sense of humor about her brother portraying her as a fictitious character. Without her, the middle section of this book wouldn't exist (she wrote the chapter "On the Nature of Stars"), nor would "The Worm of Kulkaras," which was born out of a conversation we once had about a rather unsuccessful movie. She was also my first-pass reader and helped edit all the stories in this collection, and they are much improved as a result, especially "A Fork in the Road." Thanks, Sis! You always push me to grow as a writer.

My assistant, Immanuela Meijer, for building me an Inheritance-themed wiki (woo-hoo!), her thoughtful editing, and doing such a beautiful job colorizing the map at the beginning of this book.

My literary agent, Simon Lipskar, who has been not only a friend but a powerful advocate for my work. A heartfelt thank-you! Next time, sushi is on me.

My editor, Michelle Frey, who did her usual bang-up job in shaping this book into something respectable. It was a pleasure to once again face down some deadlines with you! And thanks for helping me to finally master Track Changes.

Also at Knopf: Barbara Marcus, head of Random House Children's Books. Judith Haut, associate publisher of Random House Children's Books. Executive copy editor Artie Bennett, cruciverbalist and word-wrangler extraordinaire. Director of copyediting Alison Kolani for her sharp-eyed suggestions. Marisa DiNovis, assistant editor. Art director Isabel Warren-Lynch and her team, who made this book look so beautiful. John Jude Palencar, who painted the amazing cover. Seriously, just look at it! Dominique Cimina, publicity and communications director at Random House Children's Books, and Aisha Cloud, publicity manager, and all the rest of the awesome marketing and publicity crew, as well as everyone else at Random House who helped make this book happen. You have my profound gratitude! I'd also like to acknowledge former Knopf publishing director Jennifer Brown for her support.

A special mention goes out to fellow author Fran Wilde, who was kind enough to read an early version of "The Worm of Kulkaras" and provide me with some useful feedback. Thanks, Fran! I owe you one.

And of course . . . the biggest thanks of all go to *you*, the reader. Without your support throughout the years, none of this would have been possible.

As the elves would say, "Atra esterní ono thelduin." Or, "May good fortune rule over you."

Christopher Paolini
December 2018

From Angela:

This book only exists because of all the exemplary people Christopher already thanked. Those who particularly helped with my small contribution to the story are:

My parents! I would not be who I am today without their care, dedication, and love. Huge thanks to my mother for her insightful editorial remarks.

Christopher, for his tireless work creating the land of Alagaësia and so many new worlds that readers will soon get to visit. He kindly invited me to play with his characters and, once again, lend my voice to Angela the herbalist, this time in prose, not just dialogue.

Immanuela Meijer, for her daily work on everything Paolini, as well as her incomparable depth of knowledge of Christopher's invented lands.

She keeps new stories consistent with all the details of past tales.

All the hardworking people at PRH, whose speedy responses brought this book to your hands just months after its inception. Special thanks to Michelle Frey, who is not only the stalwart editor of all things Alagaësia but also a wonderful, kind person and a dear friend.

Simon Lipskar, for his incomparable knowledge of the business of publishing and fierce defense of the work.

And my dear Caru, who worked by my side as I wrote this story; you are a good bean.

Angela Paolini
December 2018

READ THE FIRST CHAPTER OF

ERAGON

BOOK ONE IN THE INHERITANCE CYCLE

PROLOGUE:
SHADE OF FEAR

Wind howled through the night, carrying a scent that would change the world. A tall Shade lifted his head and sniffed the air. He looked human except for his crimson hair and maroon eyes.

He blinked in surprise. The message had been correct: they were here. Or was it a trap? He weighed the odds, then said icily, "Spread out; hide behind trees and bushes. Stop whoever is coming . . . or die."

Around him shuffled twelve Urgals with short swords and round iron shields painted with black symbols. They resembled men with bowed legs and thick, brutish arms made for crushing. A pair of twisted horns grew above their small ears. The monsters hurried into the brush, grunting as they hid. Soon the rustling quieted and the forest was silent again.

The Shade peered around a thick tree and looked up the trail. It was too dark for any human to see, but for him the faint moonlight was like sunshine streaming between the trees; every detail was clear and sharp to his searching gaze. He remained unnaturally quiet, a long pale sword in his hand. A wire-thin scratch curved down the blade. The weapon was thin enough to slip between a pair of ribs, yet stout enough to hack through the hardest armor.

The Urgals could not see as well as the Shade; they groped like blind beggars, fumbling with their weapons. An owl screeched, cutting through the silence. No one relaxed until the bird flew past. Then the monsters shivered in the cold night; one snapped a twig with his heavy boot. The Shade hissed in anger, and the Urgals shrank back, motionless. He suppressed his distaste—they smelled like fetid meat—and turned away. They were tools, nothing more.

The Shade forced back his impatience as the minutes became hours. The scent must have wafted far ahead of its owners. He did not let the Urgals get up or warm themselves. He denied himself those luxuries, too, and stayed behind the tree, watching the trail. Another gust of wind rushed through the forest. The smell was stronger this time. Excited, he lifted a thin lip in a snarl.

"Get ready," he whispered, his whole body vibrating. The tip of his sword moved in small circles. It had taken many plots and much pain to bring himself to this moment. It would not do to lose control now.

Eyes brightened under the Urgals' thick brows, and the creatures gripped their weapons tighter. Ahead of them, the Shade heard a clink as something hard struck a loose stone. Faint smudges emerged from the darkness and advanced down the trail.

Three white horses with riders cantered toward the ambush, their heads held high and proud, their coats rippling in the moonlight like liquid silver.

On the first horse was an elf with pointed ears and elegantly slanted eyebrows. His build was slim but strong, like a rapier. A powerful bow was slung on his back. A sword pressed against his side opposite a quiver of arrows fletched with swan feathers.

The last rider had the same fair face and angled features as the other. He carried a long spear in his right hand and a white dagger at his belt. A helm of extraordinary craftsmanship, wrought with amber and gold, rested on his head.

Between these two rode a raven-haired elven lady, who surveyed her surroundings with poise. Framed by long black locks, her deep eyes shone with a driving force. Her clothes were unadorned, yet her beauty was undiminished. At her side was a sword, and on her back a long bow with a quiver. She carried in her lap a pouch that she frequently looked at, as if to reassure herself that it was still there.

One of the elves spoke quietly, but the Shade could not hear what was said. The lady answered with obvious authority, and her guards switched places. The one wearing the helm took the lead, shifting his spear to a readier grip. They passed the Shade's hiding place and the first few Urgals without suspicion.

The Shade was already savoring his victory when the wind changed direction and swept toward the elves, heavy with the Urgals' stench. The horses snorted with alarm and tossed their heads. The riders stiffened, eyes flashing from side to side, then wheeled their mounts around and galloped away.

The lady's horse surged forward, leaving her guards far behind. Forsaking their hiding, the Urgals stood and released a stream of black arrows. The Shade jumped out from behind the tree, raised his right hand, and shouted, "Garjzla!"

A red bolt flashed from his palm toward the elven lady, illuminating the trees with a bloody light. It struck her steed, and the horse toppled with a high-pitched squeal, plowing into the ground chest-first. She leapt off the animal with inhuman speed, landed lightly, then glanced back for her guards.

The Urgals' deadly arrows quickly brought down the two elves. They fell from the noble horses, blood pooling in the dirt. As the Urgals rushed to the slain elves, the Shade screamed, "After her! She is the one I want!" The monsters grunted and rushed down the trail.

A cry tore from the elf's lips as she saw her dead companions. She took a step toward them, then cursed her enemies and bounded into the forest.

While the Urgals crashed through the trees, the Shade climbed a piece of granite that jutted above them. From his perch he could see all of the surrounding forest. He raised his hand and uttered, "Istalrí boetk!" and a quarter-mile section of the forest exploded into flames. Grimly he burned one section after another until there was a ring of fire, a half-league across, around the ambush site. The flames looked like a molten crown resting on the forest. Satisfied, he watched the ring carefully, in case it should falter.

3

The band of fire thickened, contracting the area the Urgals had to search. Suddenly, the Shade heard shouts and a coarse scream. Through the trees he saw three of his charges fall in a pile, mortally wounded. He caught a glimpse of the elf running from the remaining Urgals.

She fled toward the craggy piece of granite at a tremendous speed. The Shade examined the ground twenty feet below, then jumped and landed nimbly in front of her. She skidded around and sped back to the trail. Black Urgal blood dripped from her sword, staining the pouch in her hand.

The horned monsters came out of the forest and hemmed her in, blocking the only escape routes. Her head whipped around as she tried to find a way out. Seeing none, she drew herself up with regal disdain. The Shade approached her with a raised hand, allowing himself to enjoy her helplessness.

"Get her."

As the Urgals surged forward, the elf pulled open the pouch, reached into it, and then let it drop to the ground. In her hands was a large sapphire stone that reflected the angry light of the fires. She raised it over her head, lips forming frantic words. Desperate, the Shade barked, "Garjzla!"

A ball of red flame sprang from his hand and flew toward the elf, fast as an arrow. But he was too late. A flash of emerald light briefly illuminated the forest, and the stone vanished. Then the red fire smote her and she collapsed.

The Shade howled in rage and stalked forward, flinging his sword at a tree. It passed halfway through the trunk, where it stuck, quivering. He shot nine bolts of energy from his palm—which killed the Urgals instantly—then ripped his sword free and strode to the elf.

Prophecies of revenge, spoken in a wretched language only he knew, rolled from his tongue. He clenched his thin hands and glared at the sky. The cold stars stared back, unwinking, otherworldly watchers. Disgust curled his lip before he turned back to the unconscious elf.

4

Her beauty, which would have entranced any mortal man, held no charm for him. He confirmed that the stone was gone, then retrieved his horse from its hiding place among the trees. After tying the elf onto the saddle, he mounted the charger and made his way out of the woods.

He quenched the fires in his path but left the rest to burn.

DISCOVERY

Eragon knelt in a bed of trampled reed grass and scanned the tracks with a practiced eye. The prints told him that the deer had been in the meadow only a half-hour before. Soon they would bed down. His target, a small doe with a pronounced limp in her left forefoot, was still with the herd. He was amazed she had made it so far without a wolf or bear catching her.

The sky was clear and dark, and a slight breeze stirred the air. A silvery cloud drifted over the mountains that surrounded him, its edges glowing with ruddy light cast from the harvest moon cradled between two peaks. Streams flowed down the mountains from stolid glaciers and glistening snowpacks. A brooding mist crept along the valley's floor, almost thick enough to obscure his feet.

Eragon was fifteen, less than a year from manhood. Dark eyebrows rested above his intense brown eyes. His clothes were worn from work. A hunting knife with a bone handle was sheathed at his belt, and a buckskin tube protected his yew bow from the mist. He carried a wood-frame pack.

The deer had led him deep into the Spine, a range of untamed mountains that extended up and down the land of Alagaësia. Strange tales and men often came from those mountains, usually boding ill. Despite that, Eragon did not fear the Spine—he was the only hunter near Carvahall who dared track game deep into its craggy recesses.

It was the third night of the hunt, and his food was half gone. If he did not fell the doe, he would be forced to return home empty-handed. His family needed the meat for the rapidly approaching winter and could not afford to buy it in Carvahall.

Eragon stood with quiet assurance in the dusky moonlight, then strode into the forest toward a glen where he was sure the deer would rest. The trees blocked the sky from view and cast feathery shadows on the ground. He looked at the tracks only occasionally; he knew the way.

At the glen, he strung his bow with a sure touch, then drew three arrows and nocked one, holding the others in his left hand. The moonlight revealed twenty or so motionless lumps where the deer lay in the grass. The doe he wanted was at the edge of the herd, her left foreleg stretched out awkwardly.

Eragon slowly crept closer, keeping the bow ready. All his work of the past three days had led to this moment. He took a last steadying breath and—an explosion shattered the night.

The herd bolted. Eragon lunged forward, racing through the grass as a fiery wind surged past his cheek. He slid to a stop and loosed an arrow at the bounding doe. It missed by a finger's breadth and hissed into darkness. He cursed and spun around, instinctively nocking another arrow.

Behind him, where the deer had been, smoldered a large circle of grass and trees. Many of the pines stood bare of their needles. The grass outside the charring was flattened. A wisp of smoke curled in the air, carrying a burnt smell. In the center of the blast radius lay a polished blue stone. Mist snaked across the scorched area and swirled insubstantial tendrils over the stone.

Eragon watched for danger for several long minutes, but the only thing that moved was the mist. Cautiously, he released the tension from his bow and moved forward. Moonlight cast him in pale shadow as he stopped before the stone. He nudged it with an arrow, then jumped back. Nothing happened, so he warily picked it up.

Nature had never polished a stone as smooth as this one. Its flawless surface was dark blue, except for thin veins of white that spiderwebbed across it. The stone was cool and frictionless under his fingers, like hardened silk. Oval and about a foot long, it weighed several pounds, though it felt lighter than it should have.

Eragon found the stone both beautiful and frightening. *Where did it come from? Does it have a purpose?* Then a more disturbing thought came to him: *Was it sent here by accident, or am I meant to have it?* If he had learned anything from the old stories, it was to treat magic, and those who used it, with great caution.

But what should I do with the stone? It would be tiresome to carry, and there was a chance it was dangerous. It might be better to leave it behind. A flicker of indecision ran through him, and he almost dropped it, but something stayed his hand. *At the very least, it might pay for some food,* he decided with a shrug, tucking the stone into his pack.

The glen was too exposed to make a safe camp, so he slipped back into the forest and spread his bedroll beneath the upturned roots of a fallen tree. After a cold dinner of bread and cheese, he wrapped himself in blankets and fell asleep, pondering what had occurred.

PALANCAR VALLEY

The sun rose the next morning with a glorious conflagration of pink and yellow. The air was fresh, sweet, and very cold. Ice edged the streams, and small pools were completely frozen over. After a breakfast of porridge, Eragon returned to the glen and examined the charred area. The morning light revealed no new details, so he started for home.

The rough game trail was faintly worn and, in places, non-existent. Because it had been forged by animals, it often back-tracked and took long detours. Yet for all its flaws, it was still the fastest way out of the mountains.

The Spine was one of the only places that King Galbatorix could not call his own. Stories were still told about how half his army disappeared after marching into its ancient forest. A cloud of misfortune and bad luck seemed to hang over it. Though the trees grew tall and the sky shone brightly, few people could stay in the Spine for long without suffering an accident. Eragon was one of those few—not through any particular gift, it seemed to him, but because of persistent vigilance and sharp reflexes. He had hiked in the mountains for years, yet he was still wary of them. Every time he thought they had surrendered their secrets, something happened to upset his understanding of them—like the stone's appearance.

He kept up a brisk pace, and the leagues steadily disappeared. In late evening he arrived at the edge of a precipitous ravine. The Anora River rushed by far below, heading to Palancar Valley.

Gorged with hundreds of tiny streams, the river was a brute force, battling against the rocks and boulders that barred its way. A low rumble filled the air.

He camped in a thicket near the ravine and watched the moonrise before going to bed.

It grew colder over the next day and a half. Eragon traveled quickly and saw little of the wary wildlife. A bit past noon, he heard the Igualda Falls blanketing everything with the dull sound of a thousand splashes. The trail led him onto a moist slate outcropping, which the river sped past, flinging itself into empty air and down mossy cliffs.

Before him lay Palancar Valley, exposed like an unrolled map. The base of the Igualda Falls, more than a half-mile below, was the northernmost point of the valley. A little ways from the falls was Carvahall, a cluster of brown buildings. White smoke rose from the chimneys, defiant of the wilderness around it. At this height, farms were small square patches no bigger than the end of his finger. The land around them was tan or sandy, where dead grass swayed in the wind. The Anora River wound from the falls toward Palancar's southern end, reflecting great strips of sunlight. Far in the distance it flowed past the village Therinsford and the lonely mountain Utgard. Beyond that, he knew only that it turned north and ran to the sea.

After a pause, Eragon left the outcropping and started down the trail, grimacing at the descent. When he arrived at the bottom, soft dusk was creeping over everything, blurring colors and shapes into gray masses. Carvahall's lights shimmered nearby in the twilight; the houses cast long shadows. Aside from Therinsford, Carvahall was the only village in Palancar Valley. The settlement was secluded and surrounded by harsh, beautiful land. Few traveled here except merchants and trappers.

The village was composed of stout log buildings with low roofs— some thatched, others shingled. Smoke billowed from the chimneys, giving the air a woody smell. The buildings had wide porches where people gathered to talk and conduct business. Occasionally a window brightened as a candle or lamp was lit. Eragon heard men talking loudly in the evening air while wives scurried to fetch their husbands, scolding them for being late.

Eragon wove his way between the houses to the butcher's shop, a broad, thick-beamed building. Overhead, the chimney belched black smoke.

He pushed the door open. The spacious room was warm and well lit by a fire snapping in a stone fireplace. A bare counter stretched across the far side of the room. The floor was strewn with loose straw. Everything was scrupulously clean, as if the owner spent his leisure time digging in obscure crannies for minuscule pieces of filth. Behind the counter stood the butcher Sloan. A small man, he wore a cotton shirt and a long, bloodstained smock. An impressive array of knives swung from his belt. He had a sallow, pockmarked face, and his black eyes were suspicious. He polished the counter with a ragged cloth.

Sloan's mouth twisted as Eragon entered. "Well, the mighty hunter joins the rest of us mortals. How many did you bag this time?"

"None," was Eragon's curt reply. He had never liked Sloan. The butcher always treated him with disdain, as if he were something unclean. A widower, Sloan seemed to care for only one person—his daughter, Katrina, on whom he doted.

"I'm amazed," said Sloan with affected astonishment. He turned his back on Eragon to scrape something off the wall. "And that's your reason for coming here?"

"Yes," admitted Eragon uncomfortably.

"If that's the case, let's see your money." Sloan tapped his fingers when Eragon shifted his feet and remained silent. "Come on—either you have it or you don't. Which is it?"

"I don't really have any money, but I do—"

"What, no money?" the butcher cut him off sharply. "And you expect to buy meat! Are the other merchants giving away their wares? Should I just hand you the goods without charge? Besides," he said abruptly, "it's late. Come back tomorrow with money. I'm closed for the day."

Eragon glared at him. "I can't wait until tomorrow, Sloan. It'll be worth your while, though; I found something to pay you with." He pulled out the stone with a flourish and set it gently on the scarred counter, where it gleamed with light from the dancing flames.

"Stole it is more likely," muttered Sloan, leaning forward with an interested expression.

Ignoring the comment, Eragon asked, "Will this be enough?"

Sloan picked up the stone and gauged its weight speculatively. He ran his hands over its smoothness and inspected the white veins. With a calculating look, he set it down. "It's pretty, but how much is it worth?"

"I don't know," admitted Eragon, "but no one would have gone to the trouble of shaping it unless it had some value."

"Obviously," said Sloan with exaggerated patience. "But how much value? Since you don't know, I suggest that you find a trader who does, or take my offer of three crowns."

"That's a miser's bargain! It must be worth at least ten times that," protested Eragon. Three crowns would not even buy enough meat to last a week.

Sloan shrugged. "If you don't like my offer, wait until the traders arrive. Either way, I'm tired of this conversation."

The traders were a nomadic group of merchants and entertainers who visited Carvahall every spring and winter. They bought whatever excess the villagers and local farmers had managed to grow or make, and sold what they needed to live through another year: seeds, animals, fabric, and supplies like salt and sugar.

But Eragon did not want to wait until they arrived; it could be a while, and his family needed the meat now. "Fine, I accept," he snapped.

"Good, I'll get you the meat. Not that it matters, but where did you find this?"

"Two nights ago in the Spine—"

"Get out!" demanded Sloan, pushing the stone away. He stomped furiously to the end of the counter and started scrubbing old bloodstains off a knife.

"Why?" asked Eragon. He drew the stone closer, as if to protect it from Sloan's wrath.

"I won't deal with anything you bring back from those damned mountains! Take your sorcerer's stone elsewhere." Sloan's hand suddenly slipped and he cut a finger on the knife, but he seemed not to notice. He continued to scrub, staining the blade with fresh blood.

"You refuse to sell to me!"

"Yes! Unless you pay with coins," Sloan growled, and hefted the knife, sidling away. "Go, before I make you!"

The door behind them slammed open. Eragon whirled around, ready for more trouble. In stomped Horst, a hulking man. Sloan's daughter, Katrina—a tall girl of sixteen—trailed behind him with a determined expression. Eragon was surprised to see her; she usually absented herself from any arguments involving her father. Sloan glanced at them warily, then started to accuse Eragon. "He won't—"

"Quiet," announced Horst in a rumbling voice, cracking his knuckles at the same time. He was Carvahall's smith, as his thick neck and scarred leather apron attested. His powerful arms were bare to the elbow; a great expanse of hairy muscular chest was visible through the top of his shirt. A black beard, carelessly trimmed, roiled and knotted like his jaw muscles. "Sloan, what have you done now?"

"Nothing." He gave Eragon a murderous gaze, then spat, "This . . . *boy* came in here and started badgering me. I asked him to leave, but he won't budge. I even threatened him and he still ignored me!" Sloan seemed to shrink as he looked at Horst.

"Is this true?" demanded the smith.

"No!" replied Eragon. "I offered this stone as payment for some meat, and he accepted it. When I told him that I'd found it in the

Spine, he refused to even touch it. What difference does it make where it came from?"

Horst looked at the stone curiously, then returned his attention to the butcher. "Why won't you trade with him, Sloan? I've no love for the Spine myself, but if it's a question of the stone's worth, I'll back it with my own money."

The question hung in the air for a moment. Then Sloan licked his lips and said, "This is my own store. I can do whatever I want."

Katrina stepped out from behind Horst and tossed back her auburn hair like a spray of molten copper. "Father, Eragon *is* willing to pay. Give him the meat, and then we can have supper."

Sloan's eyes narrowed dangerously. "Go back to the house; this is none of your business. . . . I said *go!*" Katrina's face hardened, then she marched out of the room with a stiff back.

Eragon watched with disapproval but dared not interfere. Horst tugged at his beard before saying reproachfully, "Fine, you can deal with me. What were you going to get, Eragon?" His voice reverberated through the room.

"As much as I could."

Horst pulled out a purse and counted out a pile of coins. "Give me your best roasts and steaks. Make sure that it's enough to fill Eragon's pack." The butcher hesitated, his gaze darting between Horst and Eragon. "Not selling to me would be a very bad idea," stated Horst.

Glowering venomously, Sloan slipped into the back room. A frenzy of chopping, wrapping, and low cursing reached them. After several uncomfortable minutes, he returned with an armful of wrapped meat. His face was expressionless as he accepted Horst's money, then proceeded to clean his knife, pretending that they were not there.

Horst scooped up the meat and walked outside. Eragon hurried behind him, carrying his pack and the stone. The crisp night air rolled over their faces, refreshing after the stuffy shop.

"Thank you, Horst. Uncle Garrow will be pleased."

Horst laughed quietly. "Don't thank me. I've wanted to do that for a long time. Sloan's a vicious troublemaker; it does him good to be humbled. Katrina heard what was happening and ran to fetch me. Good thing I came—the two of you were almost at blows. Unfortunately, I doubt he'll serve you or any of your family the next time you go in there, even if you do have coins."

"Why did he explode like that? We've never been friendly, but he's always taken our money. And I've never seen him treat Katrina that way," said Eragon, opening the top of the pack.

Horst shrugged. "Ask your uncle. He knows more about it than I do."

Eragon stuffed the meat into his pack. "Well, now I have one more reason to hurry home . . . to solve this mystery. Here, this is rightfully yours." He proffered the stone.

Horst chuckled. "No, you keep your strange rock. As for payment, Albriech plans to leave for Feinster next spring. He wants to become a master smith, and I'm going to need an assistant. You can come and work off the debt on your spare days."

Eragon bowed slightly, delighted. Horst had two sons, Albriech and Baldor, both of whom worked in his forge. Taking one's place was a generous offer. "Again, thank you! I look forward to working with you." He was glad that there was a way for him to pay Horst. His uncle would never accept charity. Then Eragon remembered what his cousin had told him before he had left on the hunt. "Roran wanted me to give Katrina a message, but since I can't, can you get it to her?"

"Of course."

"He wants her to know that he'll come into town as soon as the merchants arrive and that he will see her then."

"That all?"

Eragon was slightly embarrassed. "No, he also wants her to know that she is the most beautiful girl he has ever seen and that he thinks of nothing else."

Horst's face broke into a broad grin, and he winked at Eragon. "Getting serious, isn't he?"

"Yes, sir," Eragon answered with a quick smile. "Could you also give her my thanks? It was nice of her to stand up to her father for me. I hope that she isn't punished because of it. Roran would be furious if I got her into trouble."

"I wouldn't worry about it. Sloan doesn't know that she called me, so I doubt he'll be too hard on her. Before you go, will you sup with us?"

"I'm sorry, but I can't. Garrow is expecting me," said Eragon, tying off the top of the pack. He hoisted it onto his back and started down the road, raising his hand in farewell.

The meat slowed him down, but he was eager to be home, and renewed vigor filled his steps. The village ended abruptly, and he left its warm lights behind. The pearlescent moon peeked over the mountains, bathing the land in a ghostly reflection of daylight. Everything looked bleached and flat.

Near the end of his journey, he turned off the road, which continued south. A simple path led straight through waist-high grass and up a knoll, almost hidden by the shadows of protective elm trees. He crested the hill and saw a gentle light shining from his home.

The house had a shingled roof and a brick chimney. Eaves hung over the whitewashed walls, shadowing the ground below. One side of the enclosed porch was filled with split wood, ready for the fire. A jumble of farm tools cluttered the other side.

The house had been abandoned for half a century when they moved in after Garrow's wife, Marian, died. It was ten miles from Carvahall, farther than anyone else's. People considered the distance dangerous because the family could not rely on help from the village in times of trouble, but Eragon's uncle would not listen.

A hundred feet from the house, in a dull-colored barn, lived two horses—Birka and Brugh—with chickens and a cow. Sometimes there was also a pig, but they had been unable to afford one this year. A wagon sat wedged between the stalls. On the edge of their fields, a thick line of trees traced along the Anora River.

He saw a light move behind a window as he wearily reached the porch. "Uncle, it's Eragon. Let me in." A small shutter slid back for a second, then the door swung inward.

Garrow stood with his hand on the door. His worn clothes hung on him like rags on a stick frame. A lean, hungry face with intense eyes gazed out from under graying hair. He looked like a man who had been partly mummified before it was discovered that he was still alive. "Roran's sleeping," was his answer to Eragon's inquiring glance.

A lantern flickered on a wood table so old that the grain stood up in tiny ridges like a giant fingerprint. Near a woodstove were rows of cooking utensils tacked onto the wall with homemade nails. A second door opened to the rest of the house. The floor was made of boards polished smooth by years of tramping feet.

Eragon pulled off his pack and took out the meat. "What's this? Did you buy meat? Where did you get the money?" asked his uncle harshly as he saw the wrapped packages.

Eragon took a breath before answering. "No, Horst bought it for us."

"You let him pay for it? I told you before, I won't beg for our food. If we can't feed ourselves, we might as well move into town. Before you can turn around twice, they'll be sending us used clothes and asking if we'll be able to get through the winter." Garrow's face paled with anger.

"I didn't accept charity," snapped Eragon. "Horst agreed to let me work off the debt this spring. He needs someone to help him because Albriech is going away."

"And where will you get the time to work for him? Are you going to ignore all the things that need to be done here?" asked Garrow, forcing his voice down.

Eragon hung his bow and quiver on hooks beside the front door. "I don't know how I'll do it," he said irritably. "Besides, I found something that could be worth some money." He set the stone on the table.

Garrow bowed over it: the hungry look on his face became ravenous, and his fingers moved with a strange twitch. "You found this in the Spine?"

"Yes," said Eragon. He explained what had happened. "And to make matters worse, I lost my best arrow. I'll have to make more before long." They stared at the stone in the near darkness.

"How was the weather?" asked his uncle, lifting the stone. His hands tightened around it like he was afraid it would suddenly disappear.

"Cold," was Eragon's reply. "It didn't snow, but it froze each night."

Garrow looked worried by the news. "Tomorrow you'll have to help Roran finish harvesting the barley. If we can get the squash picked, too, the frost won't bother us." He passed the stone to Eragon. "Here, keep it. When the traders come, we'll find out what it's worth. Selling it is probably the best thing to do. The less we're involved with magic, the better. . . . Why did Horst pay for the meat?"

It took only a moment for Eragon to explain his argument with Sloan. "I just don't understand what angered him so."

Garrow shrugged. "Sloan's wife, Ismira, went over the Igualda Falls a year before you were brought here. He hasn't been near the Spine since, nor had anything to do with it. But that's no reason to refuse payment. I think he wanted to give you trouble."

Eragon swayed blearily and said, "It's good to be back." Garrow's eyes softened, and he nodded. Eragon stumbled to his room, pushed the stone under his bed, then fell onto the mattress. *Home.* For the first time since before the hunt, he relaxed completely as sleep overtook him.

DRAGON TALES

At dawn the sun's rays streamed through the window, warming Eragon's face. Rubbing his eyes, he sat up on the edge of the bed. The pine floor was cold under his feet. He stretched his sore legs and rubbed his back, yawning.

Beside the bed was a row of shelves covered with objects he had collected. There were twisted pieces of wood, odd bits of shells, rocks that had broken to reveal shiny interiors, and strips of dry grass tied into knots. His favorite item was a root so convoluted he never tired of looking at it. The rest of the room was bare, except for a small dresser and nightstand.

He pulled on his boots and stared at the floor, thinking. This was a special day. It was near this very hour, sixteen years ago, that his mother, Selena, had come home to Carvahall alone and pregnant. She had been gone for six years, living in the cities. When she returned, she wore expensive clothes, and her hair was bound by a net of pearls. She had sought out her brother, Garrow, and asked to stay with him until the baby arrived. Within five months her son was born. Everyone was shocked when Selena tearfully begged Garrow and Marian to raise him. When they asked why, she only wept and said, "I must." Her pleas had grown increasingly desperate until they finally agreed. She named him Eragon, then departed early the next morning and never returned.

Eragon still remembered how he had felt when Marian told him the story before she died. The realization that Garrow and Marian were not his real parents had disturbed him greatly. Things that had been permanent and unquestionable were suddenly thrown into doubt. Eventually he had learned to live with it, but he always had a nagging suspicion that he had not been good enough for his mother. *I'm sure there was a good reason for what she did; I only wish I knew what it was.*

One other thing bothered him: Who was his father? Selena had told no one, and whoever it might be had never come looking for Eragon. He wished that he knew who it was, if only to have a name. It would be nice to know his heritage.

He sighed and went to the nightstand, where he splashed his face, shivering as the water ran down his neck. Refreshed, he retrieved the stone from under the bed and set it on a shelf. The morning light caressed it, throwing a warm shadow on the wall. He touched it one more time, then hurried to the kitchen, eager to see his family. Garrow and Roran were already there, eating chicken. As Eragon greeted them, Roran stood with a grin.

Roran was two years older than Eragon, muscular, sturdy, and careful with his movements. They could not have been closer even if they had been real brothers.

Roran smiled. "I'm glad you're back. How was the trip?"

"Hard," replied Eragon. "Did Uncle tell you what happened?" He helped himself to a piece of chicken, which he devoured hungrily.

"No," said Roran, and the story was quickly told. At Roran's insistence, Eragon left his food to show him the stone. This elicited a satisfactory amount of awe, but Roran soon asked nervously, "Were you able to talk with Katrina?"

"No, there wasn't an opportunity after the argument with Sloan. But she'll expect you when the traders come. I gave the message to Horst; he will get it to her."

"You told Horst?" said Roran incredulously. "That was private. If I wanted everyone to know about it, I could have built a bonfire and used smoke signals to communicate. If Sloan finds out, he won't let me see her again."

"Horst will be discreet," assured Eragon. "He won't let anyone fall prey to Sloan, least of all you." Roran seemed unconvinced, but argued no more. They returned to their meals in the taciturn presence of Garrow. When the last bites were finished, all three went to work in the fields.

The sun was cold and pale, providing little comfort. Under its watchful eye, the last of the barley was stored in the barn. Next, they gathered prickly vined squash, then the rutabagas, beets, peas, turnips, and beans, which they packed into the root cellar. After hours of labor, they stretched their cramped muscles, pleased that the harvest was finished.

The following days were spent pickling, salting, shelling, and preparing the food for winter.

Nine days after Eragon's return, a vicious blizzard blew out of the mountains and settled over the valley. The snow came down in great sheets, blanketing the countryside in white. They only dared leave the house for firewood and to feed the animals, for they feared getting lost in the howling wind and featureless landscape. They spent their time huddled over the stove as gusts rattled the heavy window shutters. Days later the storm finally passed, revealing an alien world of soft white drifts.

"I'm afraid the traders may not come this year, with conditions this bad," said Garrow. "They're late as it is. We'll give them a chance and wait before going to Carvahall. But if they don't show soon, we'll have to buy any spare supplies from the townspeople." His countenance was resigned.

They grew anxious as the days crept by without sign of the traders. Talk was sparse, and depression hung over the house.

On the eighth morning, Roran walked to the road and confirmed that the traders had not yet passed. The day was spent readying for the trip into Carvahall, scrounging with grim expressions for saleable items. That evening, out of desperation, Eragon checked the road again. He found deep ruts cut into the snow, with numerous hoofprints between them. Elated, he ran back to the house whooping, bringing new life to their preparations.

$*$ $*$ $*$

They packed their surplus produce into the wagon before sunrise. Garrow put the year's money in a leather pouch that he carefully fastened to his belt. Eragon set the wrapped stone between bags of grain so it would not roll when the wagon hit bumps.

After a hasty breakfast, they harnessed the horses and cleared a path to the road. The traders' wagons had already broken the drifts, which sped their progress. By noon they could see Carvahall.

In daylight, it was a small earthy village filled with shouts and laughter. The traders had made camp in an empty field on the outskirts of town. Groups of wagons, tents, and fires were randomly spread across it, spots of color against the snow. The troubadours' four tents were garishly decorated. A steady stream of people linked the camp to the village.

Crowds churned around a line of bright tents and booths clogging the main street. Horses whinnied at the noise. The snow had been pounded flat, giving it a glassy surface; elsewhere, bonfires had melted it. Roasted hazelnuts added a rich aroma to the smells wafting around them.

Garrow parked the wagon and picketed the horses, then drew coins from his pouch. "Get yourselves some treats. Roran, do what you want, only be at Horst's in time for supper. Eragon, bring that stone and come with me." Eragon grinned at Roran and pocketed the money, already planning how to spend it.

Roran departed immediately with a determined expression on his face. Garrow led Eragon into the throng, shouldering his way through the bustle. Women were buying cloth, while nearby their husbands examined a new latch, hook, or tool. Children ran up and down the road, shrieking with excitement. Knives were displayed here, spices there, and pots were laid out in shiny rows next to leather harnesses.

Eragon stared at the traders curiously. They seemed less prosperous than last year. Their children had a frightened, wary look, and their clothes were patched. The gaunt men carried swords and daggers with a new familiarity, and even the women had poniards belted at their waists.

What could have happened to make them like this? And why are they so late? wondered Eragon. He remembered the traders as being full of good cheer, but there was none of that now. Garrow pushed down the street, searching for Merlock, a trader who specialized in odd trinkets and pieces of jewelry.

They found him behind a booth, displaying brooches to a group of women. As each new piece was revealed, exclamations of admiration followed. Eragon guessed that more than a few purses would soon be depleted. Merlock seemed to flourish and grow every time his wares were complimented. He wore a goatee, held himself with ease, and seemed to regard the rest of the world with slight contempt.

The excited group prevented Garrow and Eragon from getting near the trader, so they settled on a step and waited. As soon as Merlock was unoccupied, they hurried over.

"And what might you sirs want to look at?" asked Merlock. "An amulet or trinket for a lady?" With a twirl he pulled out a delicately carved silver rose of excellent workmanship. The polished metal caught Eragon's attention, and he eyed it appreciatively. The trader continued, "Not even three crowns, though it has come all the way from the famed craftsmen of Belatona."

Garrow spoke in a quiet voice. "We aren't looking to buy, but to sell." Merlock immediately covered the rose and looked at them with new interest.

"I see. Maybe, if this item is of any value, you would like to trade it for one or two of these exquisite pieces." He paused for a moment while Eragon and his uncle stood uncomfortably, then continued, "You did *bring* the object of consideration?"

"We have it, but we would rather show it to you elsewhere," said Garrow in a firm voice.

Merlock raised an eyebrow, but spoke smoothly. "In that case, let me invite you to my tent." He gathered up his wares and gently laid them in an iron-bound chest, which he locked. Then he ushered them up the street and into the temporary camp. They wound between the wagons to a tent removed from the rest of the traders'. It was crimson at the top and sable at the bottom, with thin triangles of colors stabbing into each other. Merlock untied the opening and swung the flap to one side.

Small trinkets and strange pieces of furniture, such as a round bed and three seats carved from tree stumps, filled the tent. A gnarled dagger with a ruby in the pommel rested on a white cushion.

Merlock closed the flap and turned to them. "Please, seat yourselves." When they had, he said, "Now show me why we are meeting in private." Eragon unwrapped the stone and set it between the two men. Merlock reached for it with a gleam in his eye, then stopped and asked, "May I?" When Garrow indicated his approval, Merlock picked it up.

He put the stone in his lap and reached to one side for a thin box. Opened, it revealed a large set of copper scales, which he set on the ground. After weighing the stone, he scrutinized its surface under a jeweler's glass, tapped it gently with a wooden mallet, and drew the point of a tiny clear stone over it. He measured its length and diameter, then recorded the figures on a slate. He considered the results for a while. "Do you know what this is worth?"

"No," admitted Garrow. His cheek twitched, and he shifted uncomfortably on the seat.

Merlock grimaced. "Unfortunately, neither do I. But I can tell you this much: the white veins are the same material as the blue that surrounds them, only a different color. What that material might be, though, I haven't a clue. It's harder than any rock I have seen, harder even than diamond. Whoever shaped it used tools I have never seen—or magic. Also, it's hollow."

"What?" exclaimed Garrow.

An irritated edge crept into Merlock's voice. "Did you ever hear a rock sound like this?" He grabbed the dagger from the cushion and slapped the stone with the flat of the blade. A pure note filled the air, then faded away smoothly. Eragon was alarmed, afraid that the stone had been damaged. Merlock tilted the stone toward them. "You will find no scratches or blemishes where the dagger struck. I doubt I could do anything to harm this stone, even if I took a hammer to it."

Garrow crossed his arms with a reserved expression. A wall of silence surrounded him. Eragon was puzzled. *I knew that the stone appeared in the Spine through magic, but made by magic? What for and why?* He blurted, "But what is it worth?"

"I can't tell you that," said Merlock in a pained voice. "I am sure there are people who would pay dearly to have it, but none of them are in Carvahall. You would have to go to the southern cities to find a buyer. This is a curiosity for most people—not an item to spend money on when practical things are needed."

Garrow stared at the tent ceiling like a gambler calculating the odds. "Will you buy it?"

The trader answered instantly, "It's not worth the risk. I might be able to find a wealthy buyer during my spring travels, but I can't be certain. Even if I did, you wouldn't be paid until I returned next year. No, you will have to find someone else to trade with. I am curious, however . . . Why did you insist on talking to me in private?"

Eragon put the stone away before answering. "Because," he glanced at the man, wondering if he would explode like Sloan, "I found this in the Spine, and folks around here don't like that."

Merlock gave him a startled look. "Do you know why my fellow merchants and I were late this year?"

Eragon shook his head.

"Our wanderings have been dogged with misfortune. Chaos seems to rule Alagaësia. We could not avoid illness, attacks, and the most cursed black luck. Because the Varden's attacks have increased, Galbatorix has forced cities to send more soldiers to the borders, men who are needed to combat the Urgals. The brutes have been migrating southeast, toward the Hadarac Desert. No one knows why and it wouldn't concern us, except that they're passing through populated areas. They've been spotted on roads and near cities. Worst of all are reports of a Shade, though the stories are unconfirmed. Not many people survive such an encounter."

"Why haven't we heard of this?" cried Eragon.

"Because," said Merlock grimly, "it only began a few months ago. Whole villages have been forced to move because Urgals destroyed their fields and starvation threatens."

"Nonsense," growled Garrow. "We haven't seen any Urgals; the only one around here has his horns mounted in Morn's tavern."

Merlock arched an eyebrow. "Maybe so, but this is a small village hidden by mountains. It's not surprising that you've escaped notice. However, I wouldn't expect that to last. I only mentioned this because strange things are happening here as well if you found such a stone in the Spine." With that sobering statement, he bid them farewell with a bow and slight smile.

Garrow headed back to Carvahall with Eragon trailing behind. "What do you think?" asked Eragon.

"I'm going to get more information before I make up my mind. Take the stone back to the wagon, then do what you want. I'll meet you for dinner at Horst's."

Eragon dodged through the crowd and happily dashed back to the wagon. Trading would take his uncle hours, time that he planned to enjoy fully. He hid the stone under the bags, then set out into town with a cocky stride.

He walked from one booth to another, evaluating the goods with a buyer's eye, despite his meager supply of coins. When he talked with the merchants, they confirmed what Merlock had said about the instability in Alagaësia. Over and over the message was repeated: last year's security has deserted us; new dangers have appeared, and nothing is safe.

Later in the day he bought three sticks of malt candy and a small piping-hot cherry pie. The hot food felt good after hours of standing in the snow. He licked the sticky syrup from his fingers regretfully, wishing for more, then sat on the edge of a porch and nibbled a piece of candy. Two boys from Carvahall wrestled nearby, but he felt no inclination to join them.

As the day descended into late afternoon, the traders took their business into people's homes. Eragon was impatient for evening, when the troubadours would come out to tell stories and perform tricks. He loved hearing about magic, gods, and, if they were especially lucky, the Dragon Riders. Carvahall had its own storyteller, Brom—a friend of Eragon's—but his tales grew old over the years, whereas the troubadours always had new ones that he listened to eagerly.

Eragon had just broken off an icicle from the underside of the porch when he spotted Sloan nearby. The butcher had not seen him, so Eragon ducked his head and bolted around a corner toward Morn's tavern.

The inside was hot and filled with greasy smoke from sputtering tallow candles. The shiny-black Urgal horns, their twisted span as great as his outstretched arms, were mounted over the door. The bar was long and low, with a stack of staves on one end for customers to carve. Morn tended the bar, his sleeves rolled up to his elbows. The bottom half of his face was short and mashed, as if he had rested his chin on a grinding wheel. People crowded solid oak tables and listened to two traders who had finished their business early and had come in for beer.

Morn looked up from a mug he was cleaning. "Eragon! Good to see you. Where's your uncle?"

"Buying," said Eragon with a shrug. "He's going to be a while."

"And Roran, is he here?" asked Morn as he swiped the cloth through another mug.

"Yes, no sick animals to keep him back this year."

"Good, good."

Eragon gestured at the two traders. "Who are they?"

"Grain buyers. They bought everyone's seed at ridiculously low prices, and now they're telling wild stories, expecting us to believe them."

Eragon understood why Morn was so upset. *People need that money. We can't get by without it.* "What kind of stories?"

Morn snorted. "They say the Varden have formed a pact with the Urgals and are massing an army to attack us. *Supposedly,* it's only through the grace of our king that we've been protected for so long—as if Galbatorix would care if we burned to the ground. . . . Go listen to them. I have enough on my hands without explaining their lies."

The first trader filled a chair with his enormous girth; his every movement caused it to protest loudly. There was no hint of hair on his face, his pudgy hands were baby smooth, and he had pouting lips that curled petulantly as he sipped from a flagon. The second man had a florid face. The skin around his jaw was dry and corpulent, filled with lumps of hard fat, like cold butter gone rancid. Contrasted with his neck and jowls, the rest of his body was unnaturally thin.

The first trader vainly tried to pull back his expanding borders to fit within the chair. He said, "No, no, you don't understand. It is only through the king's unceasing efforts on your behalf that you are able to argue with us in safety. If he, in all his wisdom, were to withdraw that support, woe unto you!"

Someone hollered, "Right, why don't you also tell us the Riders have returned and you've each killed a hundred elves. Do you think we're children to believe in your tales? We can take care of ourselves." The group chuckled.

The trader started to reply when his thin companion intervened with a wave of his hand. Gaudy jewels flashed on his fingers. "You misunderstand. We know the Empire cannot care for each of us personally, as you may want, but it can keep Urgals and other abominations from overrunning this," he searched vaguely for the right term, "place."

The trader continued, "You're angry with the Empire for treating people unfairly, a legitimate concern, but a government cannot please everyone. There will inevitably be arguments and conflicts.

However, the majority of us have nothing to complain about. Every country has some small group of malcontents who aren't satisfied with the balance of power."

"Yeah," called a woman, "if you're willing to call the Varden small!"

The fat man sighed. "We already explained that the Varden have no interest in helping you. That's only a falsehood perpetuated by the traitors in an attempt to disrupt the Empire and convince us that the real threat is inside—not outside—our borders. All they want to do is overthrow the king and take possession of our land. They have spies everywhere as they prepare to invade. You never know who might be working for them."

Eragon did not agree, but the traders' words were smooth, and people were nodding. He stepped forward and said, "How do you know this? I can say that clouds are green, but that doesn't mean it's true. Prove you aren't lying." The two men glared at him while the villagers waited silently for the answer.

The thin trader spoke first. He avoided Eragon's eyes. "Aren't your children taught respect? Or do you let boys challenge men whenever they want to?"

The listeners fidgeted and stared at Eragon. Then a man said, "Answer the question."

"It's only common sense," said the fat one, sweat beading on his upper lip. His reply riled the villagers, and the dispute resumed.

Eragon returned to the bar with a sour taste in his mouth. He had never before met anyone who favored the Empire and tore down its enemies. There was a deep-seated hatred of the Empire in Carvahall, almost hereditary in nature. The Empire never helped them during harsh years when they nearly starved, and its tax collectors were heartless. He felt justified in disagreeing with the traders regarding the king's mercy, but he did speculate about the Varden.

The Varden were a rebel group that constantly raided and attacked the Empire. It was a mystery who their leader was or who had formed them in the years following Galbatorix's rise to power over a century ago. The group had garnered much sympathy as they eluded Galbatorix's efforts to destroy them. Little was known about the Varden except that if you were a fugitive and had to hide, or if you hated the Empire, they would accept you. The only problem was finding them.

Morn leaned over the bar and said, "Incredible, isn't it? They're worse than vultures circling a dying animal. There's going to be trouble if they stay much longer."

"For us or for them?"

"Them," said Morn as angry voices filled the tavern. Eragon left when the argument threatened to become violent. The door thudded shut behind him, cutting off the voices. It was early evening, and the sun was sinking rapidly; the houses cast long shadows on the ground. As Eragon headed down the street, he noticed Roran and Katrina standing in an alley.

Roran said something Eragon could not hear. Katrina looked down at her hands and answered in an undertone, then leaned up on her tiptoes and kissed him before darting away. Eragon trotted to Roran and teased, "Having a good time?" Roran grunted non-committally as he paced away.

"Have you heard the traders' news?" asked Eragon, following. Most of the villagers were indoors, talking to traders or waiting until it was dark enough for the troubadours to perform.

"Yes." Roran seemed distracted. "What do you think of Sloan?"

"I thought it was obvious."

"There'll be blood between us when he finds out about Katrina and me," stated Roran. A snowflake landed on Eragon's nose, and he looked up. The sky had turned gray. He could think of nothing appropriate to say; Roran was right. He clasped his cousin on the shoulder as they continued down the byway.